For firemen and cosmetologists everywhere. Thank you for everything you do.

ONE

Robbi

"Everybody out!" The manager yells, running through the salon as we all ignore her. She's not the owner. Problem is the owner is out of town and she's in charge. She stops and at the top of her lungs, "Evacuate now! It's going to explode!"

The salon freezes instantly, the calm before the storm. There's a sudden frenzy of women gathering their necessities, and their clients, as they run outside hysterically. I casually get up out of the salon chair and walk out with Deanna, my stylist, close behind me, and avoid the trampling stampede of frantic, high-pitched women.

We all gather outside for the details, but the manager is still in there! She comes running out with the massage therapists and their clients wrapped in robes. It triggers me to survey the scene for what stages of beautification we're all in. I mean, we all go to the salon for different things. Personally, it's how I stay blonde and that's not changing any time soon because I can prove blondes have more fun. The stylists are brushing out their hair, fixing their make-up, taking off aprons. I overhear what's happening and empathize for some of the poor women in the middle of getting services, when it hits me—I'm one of them.

The building had started to make a banging noise. The manager, Shawna, had taken it upon herself to find the problem. She was left in charge after all and the ship was not going to sink under her direction. This isn't some basic barbershop, this is Michelle's Salon and Shawna would not be responsible for damage to the custom European style decor Michelle had taken years to refine. It was the water heater. The water heater was making the loud noise, like it had air in the line or was trying to pass bad Chinese food. It was also emitting gas fumes and sparked every time there was a bang. The bangs were getting more frequent.

Which brings us to the bunch of women now standing outside in the shade of the building's front awning. It's almost lunchtime and the parking lot of the strip mall is starting to fill up with patrons to the food establishments, eyes peering at the motley crowd of women in smocks milling around helplessly. Shawna's on the phone with 911 trying to get, yes, you guessed it, the fire department.

911: What's your emergency?
Shawna: There's going to be a fire
911: Is there a fire now?
Shawna: No, not yet
911: Sorry, we can't help you yet
click

At least, that's how I imagine it from the story Shawna told. There were others calling, it would be fine. Help would show up. Hopefully. Deanna, the only person I will let near my hair, is getting fidgety and twirling her soft brunette curls between her fingers. "I'm sure they'll be here quick. We still have ten minutes before we have to wash the bleach out of your hair. Everything will be fine." For those of you who are not salon savvy, leaving chemicals on your hair too long isn't good. Hair will break off, fall out, burn. I've seen it smoke. All kinds of horrible things, and I take pride in my long platinum blonde hair. So, let me translate what Deanna said: Ten minutes until utter disaster. Others have half a haircut, shampoo or conditioner in their hair, extensions partially tied in. The people who were getting massages are relaxed, even if their clothes are inside the building and they're outside wearing only a robe.

Everyone that could primp, had primped for the firemen to show up. It's a lineup and I can imagine the firemen walking the line, *"I'll take this one, and this one. You don't mind sharing, right?" The senior firefighter steps up and says, "Sorry, I get first choice. Seniority gets perks. I'll be taking this one from you."* Anyway, you get the idea. It's a beauty pageant and then there's me with a plastic bag on my head and a lady with foils sticking up off her head like she could receive radio transmission.

The sound of sirens fill the air as the long red ladder truck pulls into the parking lot, stopping in front of the salon. The important thing here is the possible fire, but I appreciate firemen as much as the next girl, maybe more. Definitely more. I love a hot guy, even on days like today when I only get to drool from a distance because I look like a bag lady compared to the stylists. The first guy is a bit older with short salt and pepper hair. He's fit and fills his navy blue uniform nicely. The second guy is shorter, still at least 5'9" and wearing one of those bulky yellow jackets with reflectors. His face is adorable, but the jacket hides everything else–not a hint of a single ab or muscular arm. The third reminds me of Goldilocks, he's just right. Thick, dirty blonde hair and the mustache to match. His navy blue uniform pants are topped with his station T-shirt which stretches across his chest and shoulders, yet loose where it's tucked into his Dickies. I'm busy imagining the things I could do to him. Naked. With my tongue. Deanna stomps her boots and drags me into the dog groomer next door.

"Firemen? Hot firemen?" I whined questioningly, not wanting to give up my view.

"You wanna keep your hair, right?" She juts her hip out, trying to make her skinny frame appear authoritative.

I dread where this is going, but she's right. I want to keep my hair. "Yes," I hang my head in resignation.

Deanna quickly explains the situation and within seconds my head is hanging over a dog grooming tub. Deanna has the warm water on and starts to rinse my hair, but the logistics of the whole thing is a challenge. I have to climb into the tub.

I stop and challenge Deanna, "You're kidding, right?"

She looks at me unwavering and silent.

Okay, I get it, "This is so you can make a clever female dog 'bitch' joke."

She didn't laugh. I didn't even get a smirk out of her.

I climb into the dog grooming tub and I'm instantly filled with regret, sitting there thinking about how karma is getting back at me for something I did. I don't deny doing something karma may have been unhappy about, but nobody deserves this.

This was not my plan when I woke up this morning. I don't have clothes to change into or maybe a swimsuit. This is not planned at all. I haven't had enough coffee to deal with this. Today should be just like every other salon day, a relaxing two hours of getting beautified while Deanna and I exchange sordid stories from the four weeks between visits. I'm wearing my salon clothes, an old plain white T-shirt and my cutoff jeans short shorts. I've lost too many clothes to hair bleach. I'm okay with this, I do have the hair smock on, so I won't get too wet. Except, I end up sitting cross-legged with my ass on the bottom of the tub and the smock gets caught on the hose, so it has to go. Did I mention the dog grooming tub they graciously allowed us to use is in the corner window? I'm strong and I can laugh my way through anything. I'm laughing now, but I'm not big on having an audience. Did you ever have a friend who laughed so hard you couldn't actually detect a sound? Maybe only dogs can hear them? Reminds you of a balloon deflating? Maybe they popped a slow leak? They turn red and it's hard to breathe? And, they can't stop? I'm one of those, and the laugh which is getting me through this horrifically embarrassing moment in my life has taken over. The water has gone cold. The bleach is out of my hair and I'm sitting here in the window at the dog groomer with nipples that could cut glass waiting for Deanna to run into the possibly burning salon to grab shampoo and conditioner.

"Robbi? Are you okay?" I'm laughing and I can't stop. "You're turning red." Deanna was kind enough not to mention see-thru like a competitor in a wet T-shirt contest. "Say something. Now you're turning purple." But, I can't. All I can do is squeal in a tone which drives dogs crazy. Every dog in the building is barking and making the dog groomers wish we would get out. "Okay. I know what to do. Stay here." She turns back to me, "I'll be right back, don't die." She takes a deep breath and seconds later she drags the *just right* fireman into the dog groomer and has him join me in the grooming tub with a group of spectators now forming outside the window. The crowd itself is starting to creep me out because it includes a group of men that were drinking their lunch at the bar across the parking lot, ogling me like I'm a peep show. "I don't think she can breathe. I get it. Traumatic. She almost lost her hair. I'd just die if I lost my hair." I squeal, but all it does is make the dogs bark louder.

"Is she a dog whisperer or something?" Oh my god, hot fireman has a deep sexy voice to go with it. I'm done. It's the last thing I can handle and pushes me over the edge. My eyes close on their own. The last thing I remember is him shouting...

Mick

"Oh, shit!" I move quickly to catch this gorgeous blonde before she hits her head on the tub. This is anything but a normal water heater call. She's wet from head to toe and see-thru, which the audience gathering outside the window to watch seems to be appreciating. I'm not an EMT, but having worked as a fireman for as many years as I have I automatically step into action as soon as it becomes needed. This victim definitely caught me off guard. I yell for back up and catch a glimpse of the hair stylist freaking out about her customer, but suddenly change gears and start making obscene gestures at the drunk guys that were drinking their lunch at the bar across the parking lot, and have now decided they would rather watch the wet T-shirt contest.

"Rude bastards! Get out of here! This isn't a peep show! This is serious!" the stylist yells through the glass while she gestures wildly with her hands.

The words fly from her mouth while I get to work. My wet victim is out like a light in my arms. I lean my head down to her mouth and turn to check her breasts, I mean chest. I need to determine if she's breathing. Her chest is moving and there's warm air coming from her mouth, so she's breathing. I catch myself watching the rise and fall of her large breasts, unable to ignore the transparency of her T-shirt. I'm as bad as the drunks outside, but somehow this wet woman in a dog grooming tub smells amazing, and she's beautiful even with her wet stringy hair. I turn to check the color in her face and she's lost some, but her full lips are pink and slightly parted. I lean in closer to make sure she continues to breathe, and hold her close to warm her up and try to hide her transparency from the growing crowd. My mustache brushes across her cheek and she kisses me. What the hell? Not full on the lips, it's the corner of my mouth because that's what was within her reach and she hasn't opened her eyes yet. I get a faint taste of her and ignore my need for more, I'm on the job.

She turns her head from side to side a couple of times, whimpering, "I want Goldilocks. I bet he's just right." Her warm amber brown eyes open, still glazed, and focused intently on me. "Hi," she says flashing me a seductive smile, warming me from the inside out.

I smile back at her as if it's contagious and our lips meet. I know I shouldn't. I know it's not appropriate conduct for a fireman and I've never done anything like this. An intoxicating buzz between us drives me to want more. For a few seconds, I want to care for this woman who is kissing me unconditionally and remember what it's like to kiss a woman while I hold her in my arms. I get a full taste of her sweet lips and want all of her, but that can't happen. Her limp arms move and she's holding onto me around my neck when I pull back to survey her condition.

She looks around frantically, but not moving away from me. I allow her time to acclimate and she speaks before I can ask about her condition, "I'm wet and we're at the dog groomer. I was hoping this was all a bad dream, but I'm pleased to find myself in your arms, Goldilocks."

"Sorry, it's not a dream."

"Did I kiss you?"

"Yes."

"I can be wildly inappropriate, I apologize."

"Don't worry about it," I let it go wondering if she missed the part where I kissed her back. I want to kiss her again, but I can't and it doesn't matter how sweet she tastes.

Robbi

I don't let opportunities pass. When there's a sexy mustache brushing against my lip and a man's lips near mine, it doesn't take long for me to respond. His arms are around me, he must have caught me before my head hit the tub. My arms are around his neck, so I take advantage of the situation, pushing my wet T-shirt covered double Ds into his muscled chest and take a deep breath.

His hands become more appreciative holding me, when he suddenly pulls back.

"Why don't we take this somewhere more private?" I can be a bit forward, but how the fuck could this situation get any worse? At least I got to kiss a fireman.

He smiles and his cheeks are red, like a kid that's been caught red-handed.

Deanna shakes her head, "Only you." She rolls her eyes and introduces us, "Robbi, this is the hot fireman who kept you alive. Hot fireman, this is Robbi and you should take her up on her offer. I'm sure she'll repay you for your services." Deanna laughs and I shoot her a dirty glance. It's true, I have too much fun, but I don't need help here. I mean, I might as well be naked in a dog grooming tub with a fireman. Actually, that doesn't sound too bad.

A sparkle shines in his eyes, but it disappears quickly as he continues to do his job. "Miss? Or is it Mrs.?"

"Miss. How about you Mr. or..." I realize that doesn't work for guys, it won't tell me if he's single.

He grins, "Miss, I need to go through protocol. You were unconscious. It's my job to make sure you're okay. What's your name?"

"Robbi. What's your name?"

He rolls his eyes at my questioning, keeping him from doing

his job, "Mick. I'm going to lift you out of this tub. Do you think you'll be able to stand?"

Yes, absolutely capable of standing on my own two feet. "Oh, I don't know." I flutter my eyelashes at him, choosing to focus on him while I try to ignore that I could have died in that dog grooming tub.

He stands with me in his arms and steps out of the tub on stable feet. If it was me, I'd already be flat on my ass and probably in need of more first aid. If I hadn't already been unconscious, I would be before I managed to climb out of the tub on my own. His arm is securely around my body as *just right* Mick places my feet on the ground and I go limp. I want him to keep his hands on me. Maybe it's the beginning of a fairy tale. I mean, he's Goldilocks not Prince Charming. Goldilocks is better than a toad, and I've kissed plenty of them. He did rescue me and I've been told that I need the right man to save me—he's just right. He releases an exasperated sigh and tosses me over his shoulder, reminding me more of the Big Bad Wolf. Visions of me in a skimpy red satin number, both of us huffing and puffing together take over my mind. Something about this strong man's arms, thick and dependable around me, give me a sense of security. The view he's giving me is superb and I want to hang onto it, but I'm able to contain myself. He walks out of the dog groomer and out of earshot, "I know you can stand up by yourself." I keep my words to myself. He hikes me up on his shoulder and I start to slip. I reach for anything to hang onto and find my hands on his butt cheeks, where they stay until he puts me down and I no longer have a need to hang on for safety. "I need to get you warm and out of these clothes." Maybe he saved me for a reason.

"I like the sound of that. I'm in."

He curses under his breath and scrubs his hand over his face trying to conceal his dirty grin. "I meant dry. It's my job to make sure you're stable."

"Getting me out of my clothes isn't going to make me dry." Going for it, I use my sexy voice, "So, which is it? Do you want me dry or naked?" I'm pushing it, but I'd rather be naked with him than think about my morning and what could've happened. I need the distraction. I'd rather be naked with him, period.

Mick groans, the answer is in my favor. He hands me over to the younger EMT and walks away.

"Ma'am?" Oh hell no! Ma'am? "I'm going to do a quick check of your vitals and determine if we need to take you to the hospital."

"Whatever, I'm not going to the hospital. I'm fine."

"Okay, uh, have you ever LOC'd before?"

"What?"

"Loss of conscious, ma'am."

"Call me ma'am one more time and you'll have firsthand knowledge of what it's like to LOC."

"No need for hostility, uh, what's your name?"

"Robbi."

"Right, and have you ever LOC'd before?"

"What do you think?" I glare at him, daring him to respond.

"I think you're exhibiting signs of frustration and that usually means it's the first time, ma'am."

I laugh, "It's definitely not my first time. Why don't you go get that grown up man back here for me, so you can go play in the sand box?"

"Ma'am, sorry, Robbi, I'm certified in my job and the best person on scene to help you."

"Help me what?"

"Are you having any symptoms that need to be handled urgently?"

"Yes, isn't it obvious? I'm wet and see-thru, giving this whole crowd a show." Huh, "Or, is that why you're nervous? You want me sweetheart? You still like your mommy's boobs?"

He calls out, "Hey, Muffin Man," and gestures to Mick.

He saunters over slowly, communicating silently with the might-as-well-be-a-teeny-bopper EMT. "Can we release her?"

"Uh, she's exhibiting signs of frustration and hostility. Medically, her pupils aren't quite even."

"She's wet and cold. You didn't even wrap her in a blanket?" He sighs and runs back to the truck retrieving his coat and wrapping it around me. He grins at me, "Kids."

The EMT swallows hard, "She made it clear she's wet. I'll take her to the hospital."

"Fuck, no! I'm not going to the hospital. I'm fine."

"Yes, you are." They both say in unison and Mick scrubs his hand over his face as I giggle, wishing they meant I look good and not that I'm going to the hospital.

"This is my last call. I'll take her for observation," the EMT volunteers and I wonder if he's old enough to drive.

Mick eyes him in search of his motivation. "My last call, too. I've got her. I don't think you can handle her."

I smile, "He definitely can't handle me. I'm betting nobody can handle me the way you can."

"You're going to the hospital, its protocol." It's a statement made in a way I don't want to challenge which doesn't happen often. Maybe I should've stuck with the kid, I could've gotten out of the hospital with him. He gestures for me to climb into the back of the ambulance.

I stand my ground not moving and cross my arms.

"Get in on your own or I will get a gurney and put you in the ambulance."

"Counter proposal, get in the ambulance with me."

"I can't believe I'm negotiating with you to get you to the hospital. I need to go back with the truck and clock out. You keep my jacket. I will meet you at the hospital with a dry T-shirt and I have a connection at the ER who will sign you in before you get there."

"I don't need favors from your nurse hook-up."

"It's not my nurse hook-up and I'll meet you there as quick as I can, or you keep my jacket. I get it. You don't think you need to go and I don't either. It's just protocol."

"I'm not a fan of authority, protocol, call it what you want."

His eyes catch mine and his gorgeous smile shines at me. "Please."

His *please* hit me right in my happy place and I don't remember climbing into the ambulance, but I'm in it and on my way to the hospital. I swear its like he was begging for sex, not asking me to get in the damn ambulance. We stop at every light and don't even run the siren, at least I should be worth the siren. "I must not need to go to the hospital. No real concern. No speeding. No siren. Let me out here."

He pulls his eyes off my boobs, "Ma'am, I mean, Robbi, there are protocols for how the vehicle is to be driven."

"I'm sure and I bet they're based on patient condition. So, no siren? Let me out." I push my breasts together and open the jacket to make sure he gets a nice view of them in my wet T-shirt. His eyes drop. "That's what I thought."

He shakes his head and clarity hits him. "I've got you until Muffin Man gets to the hospital." He stops, and talks to himself, "Just make it easy and forget it." The kid moves to my side of the ambulance. He turns to the driver, "She's starting to go again. We need to get there stat." The siren blares and the ride gets a lot more fun. I start to clap, but he stops me and gives me the international sign to shush.

The ambulance pulls up to the emergency room and the kid calls out, "This is Muffin's call ahead," to the orderly trying to assist me onto a gurney. I give the kid the eye and close the jacket.

"Thanks, I've got her. Do we have a room number?" The kid asks the orderly for direction.

"Hallway triage gurney six."

"For Muffin?"

"It's busy in there and should be temporary. We can handle her and you can go."

The kid laughs, "I'm not going to do that to you. Besides, Muffin Man assigned me." The orderly nodded and went on his way. The kid took my hand and escorted me into the ER. "You'll have to sit on the gurney in there. I have no control of that."

I assume he's making it clear, so I don't flash him to get my way. I'm still considering it. We walk the halls of the ER until we find the empty gurney and use it as a bench. I hate the hospital for many reasons, mostly sick people and doctors.

An attractive woman with long straight dirty blonde hair stops and examines me with her sky blue eyes while she puts a hospital bracelet on me. "Keep this on. I'll get back to you as soon as I can." Her doctor's coat is embroidered with Muffin, MD. I nod, wondering about the relationship between her and Mick. She sashays her way down the hall happily and I bet she has the hot fireman taking care of all her needs.

I turn to the kid, "What's with the Muffins?"

He smiles, "Doc is his sister." Yes!

"Why do you keep calling him Muffin Man?" I say relieved that I didn't hit on a married man, again. At least that's what I try to tell myself, to cover up my available fireman giddiness.

"You'd understand if you had his muffins."

"I did give them a good squeeze when he carried me out."

He covers his eyes, "Not what I meant and thanks for the visual."

An evil grin creeps across my lips, "You don't want me to tell you how firm his muffins are?" I say quietly so only the kid can hear me and laugh.

"Please stop."

"You have any other baked goods you want to talk about?"

"Let's not talk."

"What do you have in mind?"

"Geez, do you have an off switch?"

I full belly laugh, teasing the kid that's not prepared to compete with me, "What's your name?"

"Thank goodness..." He jumps off the gurney and walks toward Mick. They have a conversation I can't hear and Mick focuses on me while he listens. I see a glimpse of interest in is eyes and like earlier, it vanishes quickly. He shakes his head and sends the kid on his way.

He walks straight for me and places one hand on each side of me as I sit on the gurney, he lifts his head and is at my eye level. Quietly, "My jacket looks good on you." My hope is back, but short-lived when he reverts back to rescuing me. A second later, "You're still wearing those wet clothes." He searches around and makes eye contact with his sister. He picks me up, carrying me over his shoulder and we turn through the hallways until we get to the offices. He opens the door labeled Muffin and sets me down. He hands me a T-shirt and sweatpants from his duffle bag, "Change. I'll be right outside."

"You don't want to stay and watch?" I ask while I take his jacket off, giving him a good view of my see-thru shirt.

"I'm trying to help you. I'm not trying to fuck you."

"You wouldn't have to try very hard. You don't want to fuck me?"

"I'm off work and I want to get this over with so I can go home."

"Sorry to be such a pain in your ass. Fine, get out and I'll change." Jackass. He leaves, closing the door behind him and I strip. My panties and bra are wet, but changing will be better than nothing. I opt to go commando and pull the sweats on, which wouldn't fit if they didn't have a drawstring. I cinch them at my waist and they're about perfect around my ass. There's no way I go braless, I pull the shirt on and it's a red station shirt with Mick printed on the left chest. It's big everywhere except my chest, I'm wearing a night shirt. This isn't going to work. I gather the shirt up around my waist and tie it in a knot at my side, so I have an inch or so of skin showing between the shirt and the sweats.

There's a knock and the doctor walks in, leaving the door open since I'm dressed. She reaches to shake my hand, "Hi, I'm Dr. Muffin. I understand you passed out at the dog groomer earlier. I've heard it was a rather unique experience, so I'm not going to make you recount the whole ordeal again. There are a number of reasons why people faint. Do you have a history of fainting or any idea of what triggered it?"

"Do I have to talk in front of him?"

She waves at him, he rolls his eyes, and closes the door. "You seem to have his number. How long have you been dating my brother?"

"I met him today."

Her lip quirks and her brow furrows deviously as she whispers, "He only calls ahead to get me at the ER when it's him or someone on his crew. So, I assumed you... Interesting. Anyway, let's do this exam. What do you think caused you to faint?"

"Mick."

"I'm going to need more." She shines a light into my eyes, checking my pupils.

"Well, you have the report about what happened. Did they tell you about my laugh only dogs can hear?"

"He wasn't kidding?"

I pretend to focus my attention on the floor tiles, "No." I watch her fidget, rubbing her fingers together, while she leans on the desk in front of me and continues, "It can get hard to breathe when I'm laughing hard, but it's never been a problem. I was near my limit with the whole situation and being on display in the corner window of the dog groomer in the grooming tub like a skank competing in a wet T-shirt contest didn't help. My stylist thought I couldn't breathe and got Mick. He said something about me being a dog whisperer in his deep sexy voice and the next thing I know I'm waking up in his arms. He was close, so I kissed him when I woke up, but he didn't appreciate it because I'm just a pain in his ass."

"Okay, well he didn't tell me the whole story."

"I get it. It's not appropriate to kiss the guy that's rescuing you, but you know... the whole hot fireman thing. I try not to waste opportunities."

She laughs, "I get it, firemen are hot. I want one of my own. But, you're wrong about the other part. He wouldn't call ahead for me if he wasn't interested."

"I'm pretty sure. He told me he's trying to help me, not fuck me." I stop and think about the short kiss. It was hot and I want to kiss him again. "He did kiss me back, but it was quick and he was immediately back to being on duty."

"His old standby firefighter line to get women off him when he's working. I've heard something similar before, though I don't remember ever hearing it when he's off duty. I've never seen him bring anybody clothes or any other woman in one of his T-shirts. Sounds like you got him thinking and he's in his head. He kissed you back and said he wasn't trying to fuck you? He's interested and he hasn't been in years."

"He told me he wants to get this over with and go home because he's off work. I don't know. I did offer to fuck him and squeeze his ass when he carried me over his shoulder."

"I like you and I'm not seeing any signs that make me concerned, but you need to have somebody with you for the next three days in case your condition changes. Somebody who's completely available and not leaving you home alone or anything. It would be best if it was one person, so they'll be able to notice any changes in your behavior. Who should we call?"

I think about it, but I really don't have anyone I can call.

"Robbi? Do you have a friend or relative we can call to observe you?"

"No."

"Maybe you can stay with a parent for a few days?"

"I left for college and never went back. They always fought and didn't want me there, they never wanted me at all and I'm an only child. I take care of myself. I don't want to be a burden on my friends."

She gazes at me, clearly surprised to learn I live on my own with no family support. She's already started to fill out my admission paperwork on her clipboard when she stops. "I tell you what, I'm going to go ahead and release you with a condition."

"Anything to get out of the hospital. I told them I didn't need to come here."

"I'm going to release you to my brother. He's familiar with the circumstances and he'll be available for the three days." My eyes get wide and she continues softly, so no one else will hear, "He needs someone like you to push him back into having a life. He flirts, but he never takes anyone home. I doubt he's kissed any other woman in months, maybe years. It will be good for both of you." She hands me a piece of paper with her direct cell phone number. "Just in case. Be good to him and enjoy yourself."

Did she just prescribe three days with a fireman? Maybe I'll get a chance to find out if he's my Prince Charming after all.

She opens the door and pulls him into the room. "I'm releasing her to you. She needs to be observed for the next three days and shouldn't sleep for at least eighteen hours."

His eyes widen as he glares at his sister, "What?"

"It's either you observe her or I admit her for three days."

I gaze at him and put my hand on my hip, wanting him to recognize I'm wearing his clothes, "You said it's your job to make sure I'm stable, right?"

"Fuck," escapes his lips and his sister squints at him ready to chastise him.

"Sounds good to me," I smile teasingly.

She laughs, "You two are going to have a great few days. Call if you need me."

"You're going to have to stay at my house because I have plans. We're barbecuing and watching the game."

"No muffins?"

"Tomorrow. Banana Nut."

"I hope you don't have a twin bed."

"Yeah, bunk beds from the station. Makes me feel at home."

"As long as I get to be on top."

"Does everything have a double meaning with you?"

"Only when it involves a hot fireman."

TWO

Mick

Robbi? I'm not sure about her. Looking at her, there's nothing not to like. She has an attractive shape and, as short and inappropriate as it was, her kiss about knocked me out. Her breasts pushed against me were nice, too. Definitely something about her mouth keeps my attention, her sexy, forward, smart-ass mouth. Fuck. I want her, but that's not happening.

My days of being a young hot-shot fireman that hops from bed to bed are over. It doesn't satisfy me. I've seen too many life changing things on the job and how it impacts families. I'm not going to put anybody through the worry of me walking into a burning building and not coming back out. Chances are it will happen one day. I made my choice and I'm married to my job, I love it. It was great during my early years in the department. I was young and could go home with any woman I wanted, and I did. I'd give them one night and never talk to them again. Sometimes they'd get a few days, maybe my whole weekend between shifts. As a rule, there were no second dates. I didn't want to be tied down. Now, I know better and I don't date or do anything with women because I want a special woman—but I'm not putting anyone who is special enough to make the cut through daily wondering if I'll come home or not. For some reason, women have a thing for firemen. I don't think it has anything to do with the fire being hot, or maybe it does. Maybe, women are turned on by the heroic side of firefighting, or the high of our risky work. I don't feel like a hero, and the risks I have to take can be stupid risky, but it's my job and I know what I'm doing with every step I take. In the fire house the crew says it's Savior Syndrome—you rescue a woman and they fall for you. I'll probably never understand it.

My sister could be up to something releasing Robbi to me. She's the smart one. Even when we were kids she'd find creative ways to get me to do things her way. She was a challenge for me then, being about four years younger than me. Now, she's my sister and I'd be lost without her. I worry her, but she's more concerned with me being happy than safe. She's aware of my opinion on women and has made arguments to explain why I'm wrong, as well as how stupid I am. She must know I'm attracted to Robbi, I blew that when I called ahead for her. I wonder if she's trying to get me laid or married or just be a PITA, that's short for pain-in-the-ass. Hmmm, I liked the way her hands felt when they grabbed my ass. Maybe I should enjoy the next few days and give her what she wants. She doesn't seem clingy, more the interested in fun type and probably not permanent. It might be okay. She thinks I'm a hot fireman. In fact, she said I'm *just right.*

Mick - I didn't want to spend my days off working

Dr PITA - Get over yourself and get laid

Dr PITA - She's willing and you might even like the girl

Dr PITA - Quit using the F word or I'll tell Mom

Mick - Snitch. I'll tell Mom you set me up with sex.

Dr PITA - She'll pray for broken condoms

Mick - Fuck no!

Dr PITA - Thanks, now I have proof to show her. :p

Dr PITA - Enjoy your company and stop being a stick in the mud

Robbi

Riding in his huge truck makes me wonder if he's compensating for something. It could be that he prefers to drive big trucks, or he's simply a kid and always wants to drive the fire truck. At least his isn't red.

He takes me back to the salon and I find Deanna. "Do you have my keys and phone?"

"Hey! Yes, I have them right here," she glances up at something behind me and I turn around.

"That's the hot fireman, Mick. This is Deanna. He's observing me for the next three days, but I didn't think he would be this thorough," I roll my eyes where only Deanna can see me.

"Are you okay?"

"Yeah, but it was either be admitted for three days of observation or released to this hottie for his days off. If hottie is an option, you should always choose hottie."

"Only you, Robbie. Have fun."

"I always do."

She smiles at Mick, "Good luck." She says the words in a way that tell him he's going to need it.

He follows me the five blocks to my apartment after I put my foot down, insisting that I can drive and pointing out that it's a short distance. I grab some clothes for the next few days and call in to work telling them I'll be off on doctor's orders for three days. I leave my car at home and he drives me back to his place, I don't fight it.

Mick's place is on the edge of town with a parking lot for the front yard and a perfectly manicured back yard with a pool, hot tub, and built in outdoor kitchen. Its party central for the station house and there are a couple guys lying on lounges at his pool when we get there. The guys wave at him as he walks around back to go into the house. "Who's the chick? Is that Robbi?" The kid is one of the guys on the lounges. He waves his hand in the air, blowing them off and continues into his house with me trailing behind him.

He gives me the quick tour and leads me into his bedroom. His room is as masculine as he is, furnished with warm, chunky dark wood. It's painted slate blue, but the wall his bed and huge headboard are on is a frosty white. The headboard is at least six feet of tufted charcoal colored corduroy, the perfect match for his navy and gray jersey covered king size bed. "This is my room where we will sleep, since I need to be able to observe you. You're welcome to use the master bathroom and probably want to because the guys are here quite a bit. There's a bunch coming over for barbecue and the game tonight. You saw a couple are already here, there'll be more showing up around the pool over the next few hours. I'll be prepping and cooking."

"Thank you for agreeing to observe me. I'd hate being in the hospital."

"It's not a problem. I have plenty of room and there'll be left-overs tonight."

"How about some cooking with me before the grill?" I lick my lips.

"I'm observing you and helping you, not fucking you." His tone sounds like he's trying to convince himself.

"Are you sure? I'd prefer you over one of the other guys."

"What?" He stops in his tracks and focuses on me.

"If you're not interested, I'll probably have other options available at your pool."

"I have to prep and get out to the grill."

"If you're sure. Maybe I can help?"

"Just relax. Maybe take a swim." He walks off for the kitchen with an irritated gait, grumbling under his breath.

I empty my bag into a neat pile of clothes and change into my bikini. It's a high-waisted black bottom with a tropical printed fold over band and a halter style bikini top that ties around my neck and back in the same tropical print. I packed it purposefully because it's the lowest cut and most revealing bikini I own. It accentuates my breasts and leaves my cleavage bare down to the band running below them. I'm not fat, but I do have shapely curves. My hips aren't enough to balance out my breasts, but you get the idea.

I wander out to the kitchen wanting to make sure he catches a glimpse of me in my bikini. "Do you have a towel I can use out at your pool?"

He's focused on prep and doesn't even turn to look at me, "There's a bin full of towels just outside the door."

"Are you sure you don't want help?" I offer again sweetly, trying to get him to look at me.

"Yes, why?"

"You're so busy, you didn't even turn when you talked me." He's such a frustrating man! I never have to try this hard.

He stops and turns, then immediately is back to what he was doing. "Better?" he says attempting to placate me.

I turn and head toward the pool with attitude, grabbing a beach towel on my way by the bin. I strut toward the pool. "Hey guys, how are you doing?" I say loudly, waving and getting everyone's attention.

The number of guys around the pool has already multiplied and they all turn to check me out as I decide which lounge to lay my towel out on. There's even a loud wolf whistle from one of them. A loud slam comes from the kitchen and Mick comes walking out. He points at the different guys. "Stop it. I don't want to hear it." He beelines straight for me and as I'm bent over laying my towel out, stops in his tracks to take in the view. His voice is low and husky, "I want a better view of your ass later, but for now..." He grabs me, pulling me against him and plants his lips on mine. I accept him, wrapping my arms around him and one of my legs as I kiss him back. He slides his tongue across my lower lip and I willingly open for him. He's hot and solid under my fingertips. His lips are soft and demanding. His hands burning on my bare skin. He sends a flame shooting through me as his tongue dances with mine and his hands move to hold my head where he wants me. The kiss goes on and on. I slide my hands down his back and rest them on his ass, I can't help but squeeze his muffins. He pushes his hard cock against me, surprising me. He pulls back as out of breath as I am, and whispers, "There will be more of this later. Now I know how to keep us awake for the next eighteen hours." He picks me up and throws me into the pool. "Cool off, Robbi."

THREE

Robbi

I swim to the edge of the pool and rest my chin on my hands there, as I watch him walk away. His ass is tasty, I need to get a bite of it later. I yell, "Hey, Mr. Hottie, you've got some nice muffins there, why don't you take your shirt off so I have a view of the whole package?" He shakes his head and waves me off without even turning around. I continue loudly in his direction, "I guess I'll have to check out the other views." He stops and turns around in time to see a couple of the new arrivals pull their shirts off and flex while they smile at me. I giggle, because I've got firemen flexing for me, and the only thing better than that is Mick.

Mick yells out, "Dino, tend to her please. I need to finish prep."

The kid immediately bounces off his lounger, with a wide dirty grin. "Yes, sir. My pleasure."

"Dino! My pleasure. You just watch her."

"Yes, Captain," with resolve. He dives into the pool and challenges me to a race.

From the kitchen, "Don't wear her out. I have to keep her awake for another fourteen hours."

I squeeze my breasts together and Dino's eyes about pop out of their sockets. I laugh at my power and wonder how many of these guys I'm getting attention from. There are nice views all around the pool and I consider calling over my girls, but why share?

Mick

I must need to get laid. I can't remember a woman ever feeling so right in my hands. Fuck, I still have a hard-on. She's so smooth all over and her tits are... I want to lick them all over and shove my dick between them.

I hear a commotion out at the pool and glance out to find everyone has jumped in. Bunch of fuckin' show-offs. It's too much for her right now and I don't want her in the middle of it.

"Dino!" I yell as I stomp out to the edge of the pool without giving him direction. I'll handle it myself. I kneel at the side of the pool. "Robbi?" She swims directly to me with her tits floating and her whiskey brown eyes shining at me. All these other guys around, mostly younger, and she's focused on me.

She gets to the side of the pool, and I reach in and grab her, pulling her out. She's top heavy, but soft and curvy. "Why don't you be in charge of the races, instead of in the middle of them? You shouldn't be over doing it today. You've got hours before you can sleep." I try to appeal to whatever sensible side she might have. She must know her incident this morning could've had a much worse outcome.

She smiles at me, the shine in her eyes glistening, "You don't want me in the pool with all the guys?"

She's right. "I need to be able to keep you awake."

"I was planning on that later," she tells me with a dirty smirk. "I like your plan and what you pressed against me." She whispers quietly at my ear and the warmth of her breath travels along my neck.

"I'm doing my job and taking care of you, observing you."

"You want to take care of me?" She asks me with a smile and giggles.

I take in the view of her in her wet bikini and remember her as the winner of the wet T-shirt contest from earlier in the day. She's not skinny or frail. Her ass and hips drive me crazy, her breasts are ready to fall out of her bikini, and the way her eyes shine slay me. Damn it. "Dino! Take two of the rooks and finish prep. Have it ready and at the grill in thirty."

"Yes, Captain."

What the fuck am I doing? I pull my shirt off and pull Robbi against me, my hands on her ass. I give her a quick kiss on the lips and quietly, "You want me or is this a fireman thing? I don't need payback for saving you, it's my job." I don't know why I'm asking. It doesn't matter. This isn't permanent.

"I want you." She runs her fingers through my hair and I feel it in my dick. Her gaze on me heats me up and I remember her lips on mine, sucking at my lower lip.

I pull away and dive in to cool off, hoping for some control before I fuck her right on the lounge chair. I line up to race with the rest of the guys and chew myself out for showing-off for her. I don't show-off. I'm not one of the young hot shots. I'm screwed, and I'm hoping it will be in the best possible way. Fuck! I want this woman.

Robbi

I swear he's showing off for me! This can't be happening.

Finally, no shirt! A tan six pack, muscular arms and shoulders, and enough hair on his chest to lead me to his happy trail. God, I love a real man with real man features and a real man cock. I watch him dive in the pool and line up with the rest to race. I sit on the lounge at the side and become the flag girl. I watch as he blows his crew away, getting to the other end of the pool with enough time to stop and turn to me for my reaction before any of the younger guys get there. He smiles at me and the reflection off the water makes his blue eyes twinkle. I smile back and his cheeks are pink.

This could be an amazing three days after all. He's interested even though he acts like he isn't, or maybe he doesn't want to be, but that doesn't make any sense. He wouldn't be showing-off for me if he wasn't interested.

They keep racing and he always wins. He pulls his sexy self out of the pool in front of me, "I'll let you guys practice and try to catch up." He's dripping wet and lifts me up from my chair, wrapping his arms around me and kissing me. His mouth is on mine, pushing the heat between us while his arms tighten around me, protectively claiming me as his. He grins playfully and gazes into my eyes, "Ready?" He doesn't wait for a response as he takes us both into the pool with his arms around me. He holds me underwater, with his lips on mine and his hands all over me. His fingers sliding under the edge of my bikini bottoms, making me want more. He brings us up for air.

I take a deep breath, "More."

He smiles mischievously and does as I ask, claiming my mouth with his and pulling us under. This time slipping his finger inside me and I release a moan into his mouth, driving him further. He strokes into me a few times and buries his face in my cleavage, licking between my breasts. I explore his chest and have my hand in his shorts when he brings us up for air.

He whispers in my ear, "Cool water doesn't show you my best side, or what I have to offer."

"I know what you have to offer, I'm waiting for you to give it to me."

He kisses me hungrily, "I need to go cook. Don't get any ideas about these guys. I want you and I'm not sharing my woman with them."

My woman. I love it and I need more now, so I push his buttons intentionally. "Prove it."

He takes my words as a challenge he accepts enthusiastically. He lifts me out of the water, setting me on the edge of the pool and kisses my inner thigh sending chills through my body before he pulls himself out with his muscular upper body. He tosses me, dripping wet over his shoulder and carries me to his bedroom. He locks his bedroom door behind us and turns his shower on. He sets me down in his shower with the warm water beating down on me and kisses me like I'm his air. The heat and tension between us is growing exponentially with every breath we take. His hands are at my back untying my top and it drops to the floor. A groan comes from low in his body as my naked breasts push against him. His hands are on my ass and thighs, wanting me, he slips his finger back into me and watches me as the pleasure shows on my face. He drops to his knees, pulling my bottoms off as he kneels before me admiring my naked body and kissing my thighs. He slides his finger in again, stroking me as he pushes me back against the wall. The shower is falling over my face and his as he bites my inner thigh and kisses it to soothe it. He licks my wet sex, burying his warm tongue inside me while he groans with pleasure from the touch. His mustache brushes against me, teasing me. It's been so long since I've had a mustache ride, I'd forgotten about its extra benefits. One of his hands squeezes my breasts, pinches my nipples, while the other moves to play with my clit. I whimper uncontrollably as everything starts to close in around me, and I hope I'm not going to pass out again. He steadies me with one of his hands and continues to work my sex. He's a master and I bet he can go for hours, but it's too good and I can't control myself. He hums and the vibration sets me off like a bottle rocket, screaming out his name, "Oh, Mick! Mick! Fuck me, Mick!"

There's a low groan as he stands and drops his shorts, his eyes leave a burning trail as he explores every inch of me. He pulls me to him, kisses me and lifts me off my feet. I wrap my legs around him and he pushes into me hard as he fucks me up against the shower wall.

"Oh, God. Mick."

"I'm not a God, baby."

"You feel like it. Harder, Mick!"

He groans and pushes into me over and over. I hold onto him tight and lean my head back. He takes advantage of my bared neck, biting and sucking. Driving me to ecstasy again quickly. I cry out, "I'm yours, Mick. I'm yours." My body shakes with the orgasm he's driving through me.

He holds me tightly against him, his hand at the back of my head as he pulls me against his shoulder and kisses my cheek tenderly. "I'd leave you in my bed to nap, so you're rested for me later, but I still have to keep you awake. You can help me cook."

I don't have words yet, but I nod against him. I kiss his neck, nuzzle in, and move on his still hard cock, telling him to get his without words. He holds me and turns off the water. He carries me to the bed and lays me down. He leans over me, kissing my neck and pushes into me, holding himself deep. I grind against him and run my fingers through his hair. He grunts happily, "We will finish this later." He pulls out and starts to get up.

"You should get to finish now." I reach for his cock and stroke it with my hand.

"Later is better. I want to go for a long time. You probably aren't used to that with the younger guys."

"What makes you think I go out with younger guys?"

"Compared to you, I'm an old dude. I probably shouldn't be taking advantage of a hot twenty-something with daddy issues."

"You just got so many points with me. You get a reward. For the record, I don't have daddy issues and I'm a thirty-something." I sit up and grab him before he can walk away. My hands on his ass, I turn him to me and kiss the end of his cock. I swirl my tongue around his tip, sucking lightly and wrap my hand around the base of his hard cock.

"You don't need to do that."

"I do what I want to do. Are you complaining?"

"No, ma'am."

"Ma'am? I was a twenty-something and now I'm old?"

"The last thing you are is old."

"You keep saying things like that and I might finish you instead of torturing you."

"We need to go cook."

"My rule book says if you give you get, and you're not leaving me feeling inadequate because I didn't finish the job."

"Then stop talking and suck me."

Something about his authoritative command turns me on. I suck him into my mouth and hum while I slide my mouth back to his tip. I glance up at him and he's watching me. I lick him from end to end and suck on him until his tip is at the back of my throat. I drag my tongue and lips across him as I pull and suck him back in, over and over. Taking him deep on every pass. He gets harder and changes his stance.

"I thought you were in your early twenties, a baby. You're a woman like no other."

I move on him faster, stroking him tightly with my lips.

He tangles his fingers in my long blonde hair, pulling it out of my face and wrapping it around his hand while he palms the back of my head. He's feeling me move on him and breathing harder. "Fuck, you're perfect." He groans and starts to move with me. "I wanted to wait until later, but I need to go hard. Are you up for it?"

I suck on him hard, he's going to have to pull me off his dick if he wants me to stop.

"Robbi... Grrr... Fuck... I need to fuck you. Bend over for me."

I ignore him and keep sucking on him.

"Be a good girl or I'll spank you." He chuckles, "I might spank you anyway."

He pulls my mouth off of his hard length and kisses me hard. Sexual need surging through my veins. His hands are on me, moving me into the position he wants, he bends me over at the edge of the bed and pushes into me, "Yeah, this is what I want. Fuck, yeah." He slides in and out as he holds onto my ass cheeks. "Hard and fast, baby. We're taking too long in here. We'll have more time later. I'll take care of you better than ever before, you won't know what to do." He strokes into me hard and fast, pounding into me with need.

I cry out and push back meeting his strokes, "Mick... mmm."

"You like that, baby? You like me to bend you over and fuck you from behind?"

"Yes."

"Fuck me."

I reach for our connection and his hard cock entering me, filling me, lightly stroking him in the process. I start pounding back against him, wanting more.

"Robbi... stop. You gotta stop." But I don't. He growls and smacks my ass. The sting is perfect and drives me further. My breath ragged, I keep going and he smacks my ass again.

"Mick!" I scream out and he slams into me over and over. He digs his fingers into my hips taking control of me, pulling me onto him hard. Faster and faster, the friction between us building to a smoldering burn.

He bends over me, holding my breasts in his hands and pinching my nipples as he fucks me. His mouth at my ear, "I've needed this. I'm going to spend most of these three days with you naked right here. My hard dick in you more than it's not."

"Oh, fuck... yes please. Fuck. Fuck. Fuck. Mick! Oh! Faster! Take me harder! Harder!"

He chuckles under his breath, "A request I cannot deny."

He strokes into me harder and harder, faster and faster, "More?"

"Yes," I cry out.

Our friction hits it's burning point and we're both near our limits. My body is trembling while it moves to meet his of its own free will. His mouth biting on my neck and collarbone. "Come hard, Mick. Make it the best it can be."

"Grrrr..." His pace changes and the strokes smooth out evenly and consistent. He's pulling almost all the way out on every pass. His thick round head keeps stroking me, anchoring him inside me. His smooth pace gets harder. He stiffens and throbs as he pulsates, filling me with his hot fluids. "Oh, Robbi. Fuck me." He takes a ragged breath. "You're amazing." He kisses my neck and back. He pulls out and lays on his back on the bed next to me. He reaches for my hand and pulls me closer to him. "Was it good for you?"

"MmmmHmm..." I close my eyes ready for a nap.

"If you want more, I'll give it to you all night long. I want more of you, beautiful girl. Robbi?"

Mick

Robbi is fucking amazing. I could fuck her for days, possibly months or even years. I can't wait to get her again later tonight.

Why haven't I been having sex? Right, married to the job. No permanent women. I didn't say anything about making Robbi permanent. I want to fuck her again, maybe every waking hour of the next three days. Maybe I can get my sister to extend her observation time to five days and take a couple days off. Nah, that's stupid.

Robbi still didn't respond to me. She hasn't shut up since I met her. Shit, even when I fucked her silent in the shower she communicated with me with her lips on my neck. Fuck!

"Robbi?" I turn to check on her and sure enough, asleep. The one thing I needed to make sure didn't happen. "Robbi." I say her name again louder, "Robbi!" No response. I lean over and kiss her. She reaches her arms around me and kisses me back.

"You're insatiable. I love it," she purrs.

Okay, no harm no foul. "Plenty more for you later." I kiss her cheek and get up, pulling her up with me. We both get dressed quickly and get to work at the grill.

FOUR

Mick

I appreciate having the help at the grill. Everything goes a lot quicker and our bedroom diversion didn't throw time off too bad. The guys make knowing faces at me, but they can all be jealous she's mine. They want her and I don't blame them. Dino about jizzed in his pants when he saw her in the wet T-shirt this morning. Her tits really do overshadow her strong long legs and I can vouch for how strong since I've had them wrapped around me. She's strong and tight everywhere. I catch myself looking at her beautiful smile and listening to her sweet giggle. I'm already getting hard again.

I shouldn't have put her on sausage. Every time she had one in her hand, one of the guys was there watching and loving the visual. Something about the way she held it in her hand, fingers wrapped around it firmly. I wouldn't be surprised if they had a private discussion about it and took turns visiting the grill to watch. Robbi had put her hair up in a fancy looking roll and secured it with a wooden skewer, keeping her hair out of the food and away from the fire. I love the view of her sexy neck and I love the taste of it based on the number of hickeys she now has. Each time one of my crew asks if she's okay they retract with a comment about her being fine from head to toe, or ask me if she tastes as sweet as she looks—the hickeys. I've never done that before, leave a mark. I've left marks, but places nobody can see and I'm pretty sure I left a few of those as well. I plan to make more of them tonight.

I never run out of sausage with the guys, but tonight they're gone quick. It's all her and I get it, who can blame them for wanting to talk to the hot blonde with the huge boobs? If they knew everything I do, it would make it worse. Fuck, she sucked my dick willingly and she likes it doggie.

Its game time and Robbi's getting tired. I ply her with caffeine to keep her awake. We all gather around the big screen in my family room to watch the game and I hold her hand, dragging her with me. My crew are scattered around on the floor, with a few claiming spots on the leather couch that matches my chair. I don't know how she feels about hockey, but it's play-offs for the cup. I need to make sure I keep her awake. I plant myself in my big recliner and pull her down into my lap. It's a bad idea. She snuggles in comfy next to me, too easy to go to sleep. I can make it work. The game is on and it's loud, I lean into her ear, "The guys will go home after the game and I'm going to fuck you for hours. You'll see sunlight before I'm done. Do you want more of my tongue on your pussy?"

Her eyes get big, and she sticks her tongue in my ear, "I'll ride your hard cock all night. I'm not sure you can take it, old man. Is eating me easier, less strenuous on you?" She has an evil grin.

"How old do you think I am? I'm not dead. Didn't I just fuck you out of your mind?"

She giggles, "Yeah, maybe it's from all the years of experience you have. I mean, geez, you've gotta be like fifty?"

"Are you fucking kidding me?" She laughs and I know she is. "For the record, Ms. Thirty-something, I'm thirty-six."

"I'm thirty-four," She giggles.

She's a real woman who wants me and her giggle echoes through me, making my whole body happy.

The game starts and I'm no longer worried about keeping her awake. She's into it. Yelling at the game and taking on my crew, arguing about the plays and penalties—and she's right. She's relaxed and has a huge smile on her face. It's because of me. Not because I'm proud of my sexual prowess, but because she hasn't taken her hands off me. She's somehow focused on watching the game with the guys in her head and all about me with her body. It's a challenge to pay attention to anything other than her mouth and the weight of her on my dick. She's got herself sitting right on me and leaning back against my shoulder with her arm around my neck and my arm around her waist. My arm is around her waist and I didn't put it there consciously. I take inventory and find my other hand on her thigh, my thumb skimming back and forth across her silky skin. Throughout the game, she leans over and kisses my cheek, sometimes plays with the hair at the back of my neck. The whole time, she has the mouth of a sailor and fits right in with the crew like she's been on calls with us. Nothing awkward about having her here with us and we never have women around when we watch games. I love every second of it.

Dino gets up and offers to grab beer. I decline, "We're not drinking tonight."

She turns and glares at me, "You mean you're not drinking tonight?"

"No, I mean we."

She nods at Dino, "I want one."

I give Dino a hard stare requiring no words.

"Sorry, ma'am, uh..." He walks away without finishing his sentence.

She yells at him as he walks away, "I'll remember this. You'll never see this again." She squeezes her tits together and Dino can't help but focus on them, just to see her flip him off.

I whisper in her ear, "What's with teasing the kid with your boobs?"

"It's fun. He's easily distracted and controllable. I bet he's in your kitchen right now trying to figure out a way to get me a beer."

I glance toward the kitchen and sure enough he's peeking around the corner at her. "No," I state loudly and with authority. The room turns toward me and for some reason I explain myself, "I have to keep her awake for eleven more hours. Alcohol is a bad idea." Nods all around the room. "And Dino was there, so he should know better," I scold him. Robbi scowls at me with a pout on her lips and I want to scold her, too. All I can do is bite her sexy pouting lip and suck on it. I get carried away and turn her to me, so I can kiss her full on and hold her against me with her breasts pressed to me. It's all I can do to keep my hands out of her panties. She releases a sexy whimper and I'm glad the volume is up, my crew doesn't need to know how sexy she is. I had control when I was younger and I thought I was in control now, fuck me if I can't control myself around this woman.

The buzzer sounds for the end of the second period and it's an alarm to get some control. Robbi must feel it, too. She comes in close for a hug and gets up off my lap. I watch her walk away to the kitchen and enjoy the sweet sway of her hips. There's laughter in the kitchen, I go get a snack and find her standing at my kitchen sink doing dishes barefoot. Barefoot, wearing her shorts and my T-shirt, her legs exposed and my T-shirt stretched across her tits. Her hair falling out of the roll she had skewered, soft and loose, framing her delicious neck. I admit I assumed one or more of the crew were with her in the kitchen, but that's not what's happening at all. I lean in the doorway and keep my distance, so I don't give myself away while I watch her dancing around and singing while she does my dishes. I'm not familiar with the song, but I approve of it because it has her shaking her hips and occasionally raising her hands toward the ceiling. She's singing the same line over and over, but as soon as I decide that's what she's doing she starts moving her head around and spouting lyrics of a ditty that eventually get back to the repeating thing I walked in on. The game starts and she blocks it out, getting all of my attention. I love hockey and my team is in the play-offs, I walk to her side and help with the dishes. "Dishes aren't your job. You're a guest."

She goes silent, smiling at me and I get warm all over, "I don't mind. I kind of enjoy doing dishes. It's relaxing. Besides, I helped make the mess."

"You don't have to do the dishes and you didn't need to stop singing. I kind of enjoyed it and you dancing around."

She grimaces, making a face that tells me I wasn't supposed to catch her relaxed and doing her thing. "I wasn't singing. I may have been humming to myself."

"There were words and I don't know the song, but you do."

She ignores me.

"Let's go back and watch the rest of the game." I attempt to drag her back to the family room with me

"I'll stay here and finish, you need some time with your guys."

"That won't work, remember I'm observing you." An excuse I can use for three days without being questioned.

"I'm fine. I know it. You know it. Besides, I'm not going to fall asleep while I'm cleaning. Now, get your fine ass out of here before I have to bite it and strip you naked."

I check everything going on around me and all the guys are out of eyeshot. I pull her back against me, sliding my hands under her shirt and palming her ponderous tits.

She releases a sexy sigh, "That's not going to get your dishes done. Go watch your game, you can play with me when it's over. I'm sure there are still many hours left on the sleep embargo."

"I like being in my kitchen with you. I could do some serious damage to you in here, all barefoot in my kitchen." I pinch her lower lip softly, "I want to make this sexy mouth of yours scream out my name." I kiss her lip and give it a light suck as I pull away, and go back to watch the end of the game. She's back to singing before I'm out of the room and I glance back to catch her dancing, too.

Fuck me, sexy, hot and barefoot in my kitchen. How did this happen and why do I care? Don't get me wrong, I'm going to enjoy the sex for three days. I'd kind of gotten over it and I didn't think I needed it anymore. Fuck was I wrong.

Mick - You did this on purpose
Dr PITA - What are you blaming on me now?
Dr PITA - You should take responsibility for your own actions
Mick - You know exactly what I'm talking about
Mick - You sent her home with me
Dr PITA - I did send a patient home with you to observe
Dr PITA - Are you saying you did something other than observe?
Mick - Fuck!
Dr PITA - Perfect, more proof for Mom
Dr PITA - How is Robbi doing?
Mick - She's fine. She's doing dishes.
Dr PITA - Is that an euphemism?
Mick - No, and if it was I would have said I did her dishes.
Dr PITA - HA! Deed already done.
Mick - I didn't say that
Dr PITA - Yes you did
Dr PITA - Now, tell me about the condom breaking for Mom.
Mick - Fuck!
Dr PITA - Seriously? There's no way I get that lucky.
Mick - Condom didn't break
Dr PITA - So, what's with the four-letter word?

I'm not having this conversation anymore. Condom? I never even considered it. I needed to have her. She didn't say anything and she's an adult woman. I'm sure she's got it handled.

FIVE

Robbi

Hockey is one of my favorite sports and I choose dishes? I need some space from Mick, some me time if you will. I'm not complaining. His hands on me are like matches striking and lighting me up. But, sitting in his recliner with him? Snuggled in and comfy? That can't happen. I like it too much and it feels like he's taking care of me. I've never wanted to be taken care of. I'm not a gold digger, though many think I am and on the surface I do fit the profile. The idea of him taking care of me makes me get warm and fuzzy. I don't do warm and fuzzy. I do hard and fast, and smart ass. Yes, that's me. Use them, abuse them, get mine, give them theirs and get the fuck out. I'm not selfish. We should all be satisfied, and I leave them satisfied. Sometimes they want more. They have come searching for me, wanting a second date and they can be persistent. I don't do second dates. I'm the dream girl one-night stand. The problem with Mick, I'm stuck here for three days. I'm usually one and done, gone before I can form any emotional attachment. He's a fireman, if I'm going to break rules it should definitely be for a fireman. Firemen should have their own set of rules. Reward for all their risks.

The crew cheers. The game must be over or close to it. I lean in the doorway and watch the end of the game, cheering right along with them because at least they're rooting for my team. I'm suddenly heated and discover Mick is focused on me, not the game. Still sitting relaxed in his chair, he can't see the television through the rest of the crew jumping up and down with excitement, and he's not giving a shit about any of it. The game ends with an exciting play that leads to a goal in the last seconds and the room explodes with celebration. Mick had his eyes on me the whole time, unwavering. Flames are burning in his eyes and when I smile at him, they flare. I lick my lips and he shows me the tip of his tongue. I stretch my chin up, running my hand down my bare neck slowly to my breast and squeeze it. He loves my neck and wants more time with my boobs. He shakes his head at me and sticks his hand down his pants to adjust himself. The crew turns to the kitchen, wandering through to grab leftovers on their way out the door, some stopping to hang out at the pool. Seems it's part of the routine and if you had one too many, you pick a pool lounger to sleep it off. A couple of the guys head off into a different direction and pool balls start to clank together. Everybody has somewhere to be that doesn't require me or Mick.

Once they've all evacuated the room, "Robbi, do you want to sit here with me and watch a movie or something?"

I shouldn't. That chair makes me happy, content to just be with him. "We could skip it and go to bed." He extends his hand to me and I go to him without another thought. His arms wrap around me as he brings me closer until he can pull me into his lap. Once he has me there, he doesn't kiss me. He simply gazes into my eyes as the heat between us builds. Should I tell him I don't do relationships or let it go and enjoy my three days with the hot fireman? "Mick?"

"Your eyes are beautiful."

I smile, flattered at the compliment. "This is just sex, right?"

He frowns and a serious expression replaces his heat, "I'm already in a relationship. I'm married to my job."

"That's not the same as a woman."

"I can't see putting a woman that's special enough to be worth it through the worry of wondering if I'll make it home alive each night." He looks away from me and continues, "Truth is I haven't been dating or having sex at all for years. I was the one-night stand with a fireman when I was a kid, but not anymore." His arms loosen around me in anticipation of what will happen next. He's ready for me to get up off his lap and try to leave, but the truth is I'm relieved.

"I was right, you're perfect. Three days and I'm out. I don't do second dates either." I wait for a response, but there's an unexpected torn expression on his face. "Are we cool?"

"Yes. All the sex we want for three days and sayonara. Is that how this works?"

"Yep. No strings attached. Just great sex and I promise to give you my all. You deserve everything you want." The problem is his lips on mine are more than sex, it's all of him and as much as he wouldn't want to admit it, he shows me more of what he wants with every kiss. I'm willing to hide the truth behind our words. I've been hiding my heart and desires behind my words and attitude for years. I'm a pro at making rules and sticking to them. He focuses on me, searching for something and I wish I could read his mind.

Mick

Is this chick for real? Can we spend three days together and walk away? I've never met a woman who could do that, unless they weren't interested in the first place. Shit. I don't know if I can walk away from Robbi after having her once. I will because she doesn't deserve the worry of being a widow. I'll make myself walk away because it's what's best for her.

For now, I'm blocking out all the rules. She's mine for three days and I'm making the most of it. I hold her against me and brush my lips across hers softly, sucking on her lower lip as I pull back. "I have to keep you awake for about ten more hours. Should we watch a movie, play some pool, or go to bed?"

SIX

Mick

She smiles at me, "I was promised all night long." She leans in with her sexy voice in my ear, "I want to mount you like the stallion you are and ride you with my bare breasts in your face."

I can't help but stare at her tits. They're a part of her I want to spend some time with. I can imagine them bouncing in my face while she's wrapped around me and grinding against me. "How many times has a guy got you off in one night?" I know, blunt, but I bet she'll appreciate it. I need to keep this just sex.

"Nosey. Four."

"Easy record to break. We should be able to double that tonight." I kiss her mouth claiming her, "You're my girl for three days and I'm going to treat you how you deserve, and better." I pick her up and take her to my bedroom while I kiss her. She kisses me back wantonly, driving me to get inside her quicker. I lay her down on my bed and lock my bedroom door. She's so fucking sexy barefoot in her shorts and my T-shirt. I pull her shorts off and take in her legs dangling off the edge of my bed. I hook my fingers on her panties and slide them down her legs. I want her completely naked, but something about her bare pussy draws me in. I lean in and kiss her thighs, lightly grazing across her sex. I spread her legs and lick her from knee to wet heat on the inside of her thigh. I mean wet heat. When my tongue gets there she's already dripping for me and I dive in, immediately drawing a moan from her lips. I rub my lip on her clit while I lap at her juices and fuck her with my tongue. She tastes so sweet, she has my tongue searching for more.

Her body writhes at my touch as she whimpers and praises me breathlessly, "Mick, oh Mick, you're already pushing me to my end."

I'm on a mission. This woman will never forget me. I'm the best sex she'll ever have and I'll give her more orgasms than any other man ever has. Time for that to start now. I slip my finger into her wet heat, slowly stroking her and concentrate my mouth on her clit, kissing it, licking it, sucking on it. She starts to buck her hips when I suck, so I suck harder and hold her down. She wraps her legs around my head, holding me in place and cries out my name loud enough for the neighbors to hear her, so I'm sure all the guys did. She doesn't release her legs, so I continue to suck on her until she stills and frees me.

"Okay, baby?" I ask not sure what response to expect.

"Yes, please fuck me now."

"Anything for you." I chuckle under my breath and flip her over onto all fours, ready to slam her hard from behind.

"Oh yes, perfect. Fuck me hard, please, Mick." She wiggles her ass in the air at me and I can't take it. I smack it and hold my hand there. "Oh." I do it again in the same place and a bit harder. She simply gets comfortable and shakes her round cheeks in my face. I push my hard cock into her, stroking all the way in and mashing our bodies together. She whimpers and I smack her ass again. Her body tightens in reaction, so I do it again. She tightens again.

"Robbi, baby, tell me you feel that reaction when I smack your ass." I don't want to go too far and I'll never hurt her.

"Why'd you stop? I've been bad. Spank me."

Fuck me. I slap her ass repeatedly while she cries out in pleasure, until both cheeks are red. I stroke in and out a few times and reach around to touch her clit, betting she's as tightly wound as I am and ready to explode. Her nerve center is so hard, it won't take much to set her off around me and right now there's nothing I want more than to feel her already tight wetness around me come. I could simply slam into her a few times and it would be over, but that's not what I want. I want her to stay this tight and squeeze me. I want her to feel me hard and thick inside her. I want to hear her scream out my name as she feels pleasure unlike any other she's ever had. "Feel me, baby. Feel how tight you are around me. Feel my hand rubbing your clit."

"Oh, Mick, don't stop!" She begs me and I slap her ass, setting her off instantly. "Mick! Oh fuck! Mick!" She screams out and I stroke into her deep and fast while she tightens further around me.

"How do I feel, baby?"

"Fucking huge."

"That's right, baby. Remember that." I grab onto her hips and fuck her tight sex hard, slamming into her repeatedly until I lose control. "Robbi..." I come hard and it goes on forever. I don't know what she does to me, but I can't get enough. My legs get weak and I fall onto the bed next to her, pulling her over to me. I kiss her deeply and she climbs on top of me, exploring my chest and shoulders with her fingertips, sending electrical shocks through my body. I'm hard again, honestly I stay hard for her. She reaches behind her and strokes me with her hand guiding me in as she mounts me.

"Okay, Mick?"

"Absolutely, baby. Come here." I reach my arms around her, moving back to lean against the headboard and hold her in place. She grinds on me, and there's no place I'd rather be than inside her. I grab the remote from my nightstand, hit the power button and "Bang and Blame" by REM is playing. I should've done it earlier to cover our noise.

"Oh, yeah." "American Woman" by Lenny Kravitz makes her want to dance and she moves her body on me to the beat, raising her hands in the air and feeling the groove. She pulls her shirt off, then her bra and flings them both away. Her naked breasts are bouncing to the beat. I turn up the volume, watching while she bounces and grinds on me. She's so fucking hot, I run my hands over her hips and up her sides to her boobs. I enjoy the weight of them in my hands and hold them, squeezing them gently, caressing the tips of her nipples. I have to taste them. I lick both of them and suck on each of her nipples, her body reacts around me to the sensation. She rides me for hours. Sometimes claiming my mouth with hers, others baring her neck to me. All the time my hands on her boobs and my mouth tending to them as much as possible.

When 6am rolls around we're both brainless, sated and exhausted. Punch-drunk at seeing the sun's rays creep through the blinds. I hold her tight to me and pull the blankets up over us, "Goodnight, Robbi. I'll still be holding you when you wake up. No alarms. We need rest, baby."

SEVEN

Mick

I wake up after only a short sleep and appreciate the woman I have in my arms. Her curves, her femininity, her soft lips, the way she fits perfectly in my arms. I whisper in my sleepy state, "You're so beautiful. I could fall for you. I'm keeping us just sex, I'll follow the rules. I can't keep you anyway. You deserve better than the life I can give you."

Robbi

I wake up warmer than usual and not alone. I can count how many men I've woke up in bed with on one hand and have extra fingers. I never stay over and if I lead them to think I will, I disappear in the night. I'm still tired and check out my environment through half open eyes. Stray rays of sunshine squeeze through the blinds. I remember I'm at Mick's for three days. His arms around me and his dick hard against me. His mustache brushes against my neck and I wriggle against his hard length between us, drawing a low groan from him. His hands move around me, holding me tight against him and claiming his favorite parts. His left hand reaches around me and settles low on my belly, while his right arm is under my neck with elbow bent so he can reach my breasts. I wriggle against him again and he rolls me toward him, claiming my lips with his. His hands move to my ass, pressing me closer to him. His eyes are closed. He's all hands and lips. His lips move on mine like a sexy conversation without words, and he says more than any words could express. His strong hands are in my hair, holding my mouth to his and not releasing me. He lifts my upper leg up over him and pushes into me. We both groan, capturing each others pleasure in our kiss while we move together. His hands travel up my back, finding their way back into my hair at the nape of my neck and his thumbs at my jawline. It's in that second when his lips leave mine and come back for more that I feel something new to me and I know why he isn't letting me go. His wordless conversation comes to life and I'm flooded with a warmth reaching all my extremities. I'm lost in sensation. His mouth owns me and our bodies move together without thought. I press my breasts to his chest and reach around him to appreciate his muscled back, holding him to me. He gets harder inside me and it drives us both to move faster. Everything else is hazy, all I know is that I need him. He quickly rolls me underneath him, not breaking our kiss. Our kiss seems to be the force behind everything, holding everything together, keeping reality out. He rests on his elbows above my shoulders while he maintains control of my mouth and moves with me faster, harder. His breathing is irregular and ragged. His heart is beating out of his chest. He pushes into me hard and demanding, his elbows holding me in place and keeping me from sliding across his bed. He pounds into me harder and harder, with so much need. I let my eyes close completely to be with him in his darkness, eliminating the outside world and simply feeling everything. Both of us on the edge and wanting to dive head first off a cliff, knowing we can't survive the fall. Light shines as my body begins to tighten for him and I don't need to do anything. My body is in control and all I need is him. I suddenly go crashing as he presses and holds his hard cock deep inside me. His thick head almost too much for me as I come around him, squeezing him hard and uncontrollably. His kiss never stops and he moves slowly, in and out. Stroking us together with care and need, not wanting to stop. He rolls me on top of him and breaks the kiss, pulling my head away from him and opening his eyes to gaze into mine. His eyes are a book wanting me to read them, but he lays my head on his chest and maneuvers so he's still deep inside me. No eye contact. His hands on my naked back, holding me there. The lights are still there when I close my eyes and my body is still in heaven reacting around him.

Robbi

I wake up warm again and find I fell asleep on Mick. His arms are around me, holding me protectively. I sit up slowly, needing to stretch and find him hard inside me. I move on him slowly, enjoying his hard length and grinding against him.

He opens his eyes and looks up at me, "What a gorgeous view."

I lean over to kiss his neck and whisper in is ear, "Are you popping little blue pills when I'm not looking or are you always hard for me because I'm special?" I listen to my words and curse myself out internally. I don't want to be special. Special doesn't work. Wham. Bam. Thank you, ma'am. Stick to the one-night stand!

He's watching me. What man wouldn't be watching a woman ride him? His happy expression changes and I wonder if he noticed mine get twisted up at my words. He recovers quick,

"I told you, I'm not old. I require no medication to get hard, stay hard and..." He halts his words abruptly and his eyes tell the story. His filter is working better than mine and he caught himself before he said something he shouldn't.

I lock eyes with him, "Three days."

He replies, "Three days."

I need to do something to recover from this and lighten it up quick because this is getting to be deep and I can't do deep. I don't do deep. Remember the last time you did deep and you won't do it again. You're the only one you can trust. They all just want to use you. They want photos of your tits, preferably with their dick between them and if you wouldn't mind, could you lick their head, too. That would be perfect and I won't get your face in the photos, promise nothing above that beautiful mouth of yours and it won't matter because I won't show anyone—the photos are only for me. Remember what he did to you? How he took photos of it all without telling you? Remember how he let his friends come in and watch when you were drunk? Remember how he let his friends have their way with you when you were passed out and took pictures to show you what they did later?

The anger builds inside me and I don't want Mick to see it. Fuck! He would never do anything so horrible. I've seen everything in his eyes. He's a protector, a rescuer. For a brief second, I actually wonder if he could be the hero to save me beyond the dog grooming tub. I tamp the idea down and don't allow myself to ponder it. Dreaming of possibilities isn't allowed. He wants more of my breasts, they all do. It'll be a good distraction to make him forget any emotion he witnessed.

"You wanna play with my boobs? Run your dick between them?"

"No, baby, nothing better than having you wrapped around me. Except maybe having you wrapped around me and kissing you at the same time." His eyes focus on me, hoping I will oblige his wish, but I don't.

It's perfect. He gives me a reason to get up and get away from him for a few minutes. I get off him and go to the bathroom to brush my teeth, "Oh, morning breath. Let me fix that."

"It wasn't an issue earlier," he says.

"I don't think we were, or I wasn't awake earlier. Did we have sex?" Good call. Make the best sex ever—sex that felt like something more—a joke and pretend it didn't happen.

He jumps out of bed and grabs my hand before I get to the bathroom. He pulls me close to him and holds me tight, focusing directly into my eyes. "We were both there. We both know what it was. We are both choosing not to go there. Don't make it a joke, Robbi." He leans his forehead to mine and closes his eyes. Pure and honest emotion radiating off of him.

I run for the bathroom and lock the door behind me. I don't want to acknowledge the truth. I'm doing my best to ignore it, pretend it's some kind of game, and he shoves it in my face. Seriously, aren't all relationships some type of game or challenge? Women go on reality shows and compete with thirty other contestants for the love and attention of one man, with hopes he'll propose after going on a few dates and maybe spending a night together. That's not love. Ever heard of The Dating Game? How about Love Connection? Maybe Singled Out? Or, how about Baggage? How many shows has the Bachelor spawned? None of it is love. If it's not a TV show, then it's an app. Tinder is material for starting a fire. Slow burn? Fast burn? White-hot burn? Somebody gets burned. It's obviously all a game, so might as well get out there, have fun and enjoy yourself. What is love anyway? It's not worth the tears and heartbreak, especially for some asshole who doesn't deserve you in the first place. Huh, I guess that's the kicker—Does Mick deserve me? It doesn't matter, neither of us do second dates. Love... what a joke.

EIGHT

Mick

I'm not sure what happened. I thought we were having a moment, granted it was a moment we probably shouldn't have, and Robbi runs into my bathroom and locks the door behind her. Maybe it's just me. Am I the only one in this? She's going to walk away, she'll be fine without me. I need to remember that. It's been about twenty minutes and I can hear her in there, but I don't think she's coming out any time soon or even unlocking the door so I can get my toothbrush. This is all my sister's fault. If she hadn't put us together for three whole days, everything would have been fine. I might have missed out on the best sex of my life, but I wouldn't be thinking stupid, doing stupid things, and have a beautiful blonde locked in my bathroom holding my toothbrush hostage. I could have her naked in my bed screaming out my name and making those sexy noises. Alright, I probably wouldn't have her in my bed the other way either, but the thought is a good one. Shit! She bent right over for me, told me she was bad and asked to be spanked! Where were the women who did that when I was younger? She's unique. I mean, women aren't one-night stand types.

What was I thinking having sleepy sex with her earlier? I know what I was thinking. I want her. Yeah, it's the fucking truth. Not only do I want her, I want to keep her. I can admit the truth, I know what happened. I don't want her to be a one-night stand. I want her to be mine for more than three days. I woke up without enough sleep and she was moving her soft warm body against my dick that's been hard since I first met her. If I was taking those little blue pills, I'd need to see a physician for a hard-on lasting more than four hours. She makes me want her. She makes me have to have her. I couldn't help myself, I needed to hold her and touch her. I'm a fireman, damn it! I'm protective by nature and trained to be. I didn't keep my guard up. I need to do better at that if I'm going to protect her, regardless of how I feel. My heart pounding and the adrenaline rush, I might as well have been the lead man running into a burning building. Keeping my eyes closed didn't block it out like it was a dream. It still happened. She's in my heart, not just my head. It's not just her body that has me wanting her. I know exactly what I did and I meant it. I wasn't fucking her. It was more than sex. I can't let it happen again. I need to protect her. She doesn't deserve to live the life of a fireman.

I knock on the bathroom door, "Robbi?"

The bathroom goes silent.

"I know you can hear me. Take your time and relax. Whatever you want to do. Take a bath. Go back to bed. I'm going to make something to eat. Are you hungry, baby?" What the hell? I need to get a handle on that 'baby' thing, too. "Do you want coffee or something?"

No response.

"The guys should all be gone. You can relax by the pool."

Still nothing.

On an exasperated sigh, "How about I heat up one of my muffins for you? I've got a hidden stash. You pick the flavor. I have chocolate chip, banana nut, carrot cream cheese and mixed berries."

I hear her shuffling around in there, but no answer.

"You know you're stuck here for two more days. That's a long time to be in the bathroom. You know they don't call me Muffin Man for my ass, right? You should eat." I lean my head against the bathroom door. "Robbi? Please come out of the bathroom. I didn't mean to make you upset." Do I put it out there? Fuck.

"It's not your fault. Damn it. It is your fault." There's cursing on the other side of the door.

"Okay. I'm going to heat up my muffins."

"Because your ass isn't hot enough already?" There she is, my smart ass woman.

"I'm just an old man living on viagra, posing as a thirty something and taking advantage of a hot girl in her early twenties with daddy issues." I walk off to the kitchen before she can respond. I get one muffin of each flavor from my hidden stash in the deep freezer and heat all four of them up, while I brew a cup of coffee. When the muffins are ready, I cut a quarter out of each one of them and put them together making one whole muffin on a small plate. I get a glass out and pour a glass of milk to go with it. I lean back against my kitchen counter wearing only my board shorts and enjoy my black coffee, waiting for a beautiful woman to be drawn to me by the smell of my muffins.

It doesn't take long before Robbi wanders into my kitchen wearing shorts and her bikini top. She'd brushed out her hair and put it up in a neat ponytail. She looks put together on the outside. I gesture to the muffin, "I warmed a piece of each since you didn't pick a flavor." I look at the pieced together Texas-sized muffin and get her a fork.

"Thank you." She sits there analyzing the muffin and sniffing it. I'd guess she's being difficult on purpose. "Do you have any ice cream?"

I check the freezer, "I have the remains of some old mint chip and ice cream sandwiches."

"Ice cream sandwich will work." I hand her an ice cream sandwich and watch, wondering what she's going to do with it.

She unwraps it and scrapes the vanilla ice cream off the sandwich onto the middle of the plate with the muffin quarters, eating it like dessert. "Do you want some chocolate syrup or whipped cream to go with that?" I chuckle, never having seen someone turn one of my muffins into dessert before.

"No, this is good. Anything else would be too much." Her tone is completely serious. She takes a bite of each flavor, grimacing with each taste. I roll my eyes because my muffins are delicious. Then she takes a bite of each flavor with ice cream and eats them all happily, even after the ice cream is gone.

"What do you think?"

"Well, the chocolate chip could use some sour cream in the mix. The carrot is a bit dense, maybe you could somehow add some cream cheese to the batter? The mixed berries are much lighter and fluffier than the others, probably my favorite for texture. The banana nut is delicious, I'd chop the nuts finer and add more of them."

"Okay. I wasn't expecting judgment. A 'They're delicious' or 'Yummy' would've been fine."

"Oh, you shouldn't have asked what I thought then. I sample recipes for friends that enter in baking contests, so I'm completely honest and always offer constructive criticism." She stops and takes another bite before continuing, "Thanks so much for heating muffins for me and letting me try all four of your flavors. They are all tasty. Yum!"

I chuckle, "Which of my muffins do you like best?"

"I like the left one and the right one equally. It's a nice

matched set. Do you have a freckle or something on one and not the other?"

I run my hand through my hair and pretend she didn't just say that. I eat a piece of each of my muffins and consider her suggestions. She might be right again. How did I end up with a hot blonde in my house that knows hockey, roots for my team, knows baked goods, kisses like sin and likes to get bent over? Well, at least she liked it when I bent her over before. I may not be allowed to again. Fuck. I've got to wait for her, I may not be allowed more sex at all. My own fault. No, I'm blaming my sister.

Mick - Why? Just tell me why.

Dr PITA - Hey Bro!

Mick - Why her?

Mick - Why not some old woman?

Mick - Maybe a teenage boy?

Dr PITA - She's the one you called in to me at the ER

Dr PITA - You only call ahead for you or your crew.

Dr PITA - Why did you call ahead for her?

Something about Robbi. Right from the beginning, she was feisty and sexy. Her laugh and the visual of her in a wet T-shirt in the dog tub, still smiling through the whole thing. I'm happy I was able to be there for her and catch her when she passed out. I've never had anyone respond to me rescuing them like she did. I was checking to make sure she was breathing and she kissed me. If I'm being honest, I wanted to keep the kiss going then and have my way with her in a private corner somewhere nearby. Her short kiss shot through me like a lightning bolt, making me want things and consider things I'd given up. I had to pass her off to Dino, so I could maintain order and not lose my shit right there. Dino knew then something wasn't right and caught a different glimpse of it himself when Robbi worked him like a child to get what she wanted and made him nervous. She's right about a lot of things. I'm afraid she was right when she looked at me and said *"nobody can handle me like you."*

Dr PITA - Hello?

Dr PITA - What's going on over there?

Mick - Everything

Mick - It's going to be an unforgettable 3 days

Mick - Best sex ever

Mick - Neither of us do second dates, so 3 days and done.

Dr PITA - That's fine if it's just sex

Mick - True

Dr PITA - But, it's not just sex?

Dr PITA - BRO! Tell me you're falling for her!

Fuck. I don't fall.

Mick - She knows hockey better than most of my crew

Mick - She likes my team and even knew some of the stats

Mick - She fit in with me and the guys for bbq and hockey night

Mick - She handled herself well at the grill and I didn't have to caution her about the fire.

Mick - She put her hair up and everything without a word.

Fuck, she has a sexy neck.

Dr PITA - She's perfect for you

Mick - Yep. Right down to the fact that I can't keep her. Perfect for both of us.

Dr PITA - You need to get over yourself

Dr PITA - Tell her you like her and want to forget the rules

Mick - No. She freaked out when the sex got….

Dr PITA - What?

Mick - Nothing. We may already be just roommates for the rest of the three days.

Dr PITA - I know you didn't hurt her.

Mick - I'd never hurt her intentionally.

Mick - It's why I can't keep her. She deserves better.

Mick - Need to stick to the three days and done.

Dr PITA - Rules are meant to be broken

Mick - I'm married to my job

Mick - She deserves a man that will give her his full attention

Dr PITA - It's a job. Everyone has a job. There's nobody better than you.

Mick - Why are you being nice to me?

Dr PITA - I'm not. You're being stupid. Just pointing out the obvious.

Dr PITA - Any broken condoms yet?

Mick - No.

Dr PITA - Too bad.

Mick - Cut that shit out!

NINE

Robbi

I grab a towel out of the bin on my way out to the pool. I walk all the way around the pool to find the best lounge chair. Clean, right amount of sunlight, view all the way into the kitchen, bingo. I hear the sliding door open and the screen pulled shut.

"Yell if you need anything. I'm going to turn some music on." Mick calls out from the kitchen. A couple minutes pass and "Mr. Brightside" by the Killers blares through the sound system, sounds like he turned on the local station.

I slink out of my shorts and notice he's watching me. I bend over to lay my towel out on the lounge and aim my ass at him, shaking it back and forth ever so slightly and staying bent over much longer than necessary to straighten out my towel. I can't help myself. I have to tease him whether I want to or not, it's a force of nature. Tease may not be the right word, because when it comes to Mick I'll give him anything he wants for three days. It's not the best for me, but my body doesn't seem to care about my heart. It doesn't matter. I'm tough and I can do this. No reason to waste the limited time I can be spending with my hot fireman. I stand up straight and turn around, smiling directly at him while I make sure my breasts are securely in my bikini top. I dive in and swim a few laps. The cool water refreshes me as I swim through it. I swim more, hoping for some clarity, but all I can see is Mick. I must be here for him. His sister told me to be good to him. Yes, that's my goal while I'm here for the three days—make Mick happy and help bring him back out into the dating world. I don't like the idea of him dating, and it's not my place to complain since I won't be here for him or available for him to date. No second dates.

I pull myself out of the pool and crawl onto my lounger. Lying on my belly I reach back and untie my top, letting it fall to the sides and avoiding the defined tan lines. The light breeze blowing through is relaxing and Mick is watching me. I let my eyes drift closed. I can't remember ever being this comfortable and relaxed.

A splash of water across my legs and back startles me. Mick's in the pool and there's a towel on the chair next to me. I watch him come up out of the water and shake his head, then run his fingers through his hair trying to make it stay back out of his eyes. He swims some laps and stops at my end of the pool, resting his chin on his hands. "You're starting to get pink."

"It's okay, I'll be tan tomorrow." I'm warm from the sun and my Mick drive is in gear. "No guys coming over today?"

"I'm not expecting any. Are you hoping for anyone specific?"

I turn and sit on the foot of my lounger topless, "Hoping for no visitors."

He smiles at me, like he's been released from prison.

"So, I didn't see any pool rules posted anywhere. Anything I should know?"

"Don't pee in the pool. No lifeguard on duty. The gate doesn't have a lock on it. Topless at your own risk."

"What about skinny dipping?"

"Never done it."

"You? Mr. Hot Fireman? Have never skinny dipped?" My voice gets higher than it needs to be.

"Nope." He gets a dirty grin, "It's only allowed when I'm in the pool."

"Why is that?"

"In case somebody needs saving. You never know what will happen in a pool."

"Do you want to save me?"

"I want to be the reason you need to be saved." His voice is lower, raspy.

A sudden heat overcomes me and I dive into the pool topless. I swim to the opposite end of the pool and come up for air. I stop and look at him across the pool.

"So, are we staying on our own sides of the pool?"

I swim underwater across the pool directly to him and come up for air in front of him. I gaze into his clear blue eyes and reach my arms around his neck, so he's the only thing holding me up. "Why would we need to be on our own sides?"

"I thought our three days might have ended early."

"I don't want to think about the three days. Let's not talk about that. I'm yours while I'm here." I whisper in his ear and tears build in my eyes, "I need to be saved from history that I can't change. You're completely different, you can save me from everything else. Nobody can save me from you."

He puts his hand on my head and whispers back to me, "I understand. Nobody else has ever made me feel alive the way you do. The risk of the job, but never a woman. No talking about the timer, just us until it can't be." He kisses my neck and claims my mouth with his. I can taste his passion and need. I'm topless, yet his hands haven't touched my breasts once. He's holding me close, like he wants to make sure I don't get away. I wrap my legs around him and he relaxes with me completely dependent on him. I feel his smile against my lips and he dives underwater with me wrapped around him like I'm nothing. Kissing me and holding me underwater with him. He brings us up for air and goes right back down again. I rub my sex against him and find him hard even though we're in the pool. I love how he's been focused on me and not sex. I hesitate, keeping my hands out of his pants and waiting for him to take the next step. He comes up for air and climbs out of the pool with me still wrapped around him. He sits down on his lounge chair and leans us back together while we make out. He snatches the towel off my lounger and covers us. I can feel how much he needs me. His urgency. He rolls me underneath him and we have too many clothes on. He slips his finger under the hem of my bottoms.

Quietly, raspy, "Robbi, do you want me?"

"Yes."

"Tell me if I do something wrong. I don't want you upset again."

"Don't worry. I won't get upset again. Everything is for you." I mean it. Complete truth.

"Oh, Robbi." He rubs his hard dick against me. He pulls my bottoms off with his finger. He gets up and drops his board shorts. He pulls the towel away and stands over me hard.

I crook my finger at him until he's close enough for me to kiss his tip and guide him between my boobs, squeezing them around him. He strokes between them a few times and growls low, "I need in you, Robbi. Fuck." I kiss and suck at his tip, he pulls it away. He kneels on the lounger, kissing me greedily. He pushes into me hard with need and there's a loud crack. He strokes into me again and again, harder and harder. The back of the lounge chair crashes down flat and we go with it. We land flat with it and giggle, but keep going and on the next thrust drop to the ground with the rest of the chair. "You okay, baby?"

"Yeah." I giggle at the whole scenario and somehow manage not to go into a high-pitched laughing fit.

Mick chuckles low and pulls out of me slow. "Let's make dinner and recover from this." He pulls me up off the lounger with him and reaches to wrap the towel around me, but I grab my bikini and run for the house naked. I turn and look at him when I get in the house to see him watching me, "That's it! I'm coming after that ass!" He runs toward the door and I take off into his house. He chases me around until I go into his bedroom and he finds me there on all fours in front of him. "Fuck! Dinner can wait. Tell me, have you been bad?" His voice is low and sexy.

"Is naked outside bad?"

"Yes, that's very bad."

"Is sucking cock bad?"

"Not if it's mine." He takes a deep breath.

"Well, I'm just a sweet little girl. I never do anything bad."

"The only thing sweet about you is how you taste." He drops to his knees and licks me luxuriously, tasting my sweetness. "Oh yeah, so sweet."

I shake my ass at him and he smacks it, "You teasing me?"

"I'm no tease."

"No? So, you want me to fuck you hard from behind until you can't walk? Until you can't even hold yourself up on your knees and hands?"

"Yes."

He smacks my ass again and shoves his hard cock into me deep, all at once.

I scream out loud and push back against him.

"That's my girl." He smacks my ass again, spanking me over and over leaving the perfect sting. He rubs my ass to soothe it. He pulls my knees back to the very edge of his bed and stands behind me with his fingertips digging into my hips. "I want you so fucking bad." He says on a low growl while he takes me completely. Slamming into me hard and fast. "Fuck, yes. So fucking tight around me."

I'm breathing ragged already and he's harder than ever before, determined to fuck me into oblivion. I pound back against him, meeting his strokes and showing him I want more.

"This is only round one, baby." He slams me hard over and over. He reaches between my legs to find my nerve center and I explode at his touch.

I scream out his name, "Mick! Oh, fuck! So, fucking huge." I scream on every pass as he keeps fucking me hard and fast. He smacks my ass and I tighten even more. "Oh!"

His fingertips dig into my hips, holding on tight while he pulls me to him. Pushing and pulling me, on and off of his hard needy length. He pounds into me and holds me against him. He bends over me and whispers in my ear, "This isn't what I want. Can I have what I want?"

"Yes, whatever you want."

He pulls out of me and flips me over on the bed. He pushes back into me and slides me further onto the bed, so there's room for him. He picks me up, holding me in his arms while we're connected. Holding me tight against him, he presses his lips to mine. It's his fucking kiss. It makes me more his every time. His lips and his magic tongue.

I whimper at the kiss.

"You okay, baby?"

"Your kiss owns me." It shoots through me and he's in complete control. I'm willing to give him complete control. He will take care of me.

"I feel it, too, baby. I don't want to stop."

"Don't stop. Just have me."

"Fuck me." He lays me down gently, propped up on the

pillows and keeps kissing me. Holding me, his arms around me and slowly consumed by our friction. Our heat keeps building as our bodies move together as one. "You're perfect, Robbi. Fuck." Mick's grip on me suddenly gets tighter and I feel him come inside me. His eyes are closed and his body is stiff, "Baby," his breathing irregular as he stops moving and leans in to kiss my neck. "Only you do this to me." We lie together, connected.

TEN

Mick

This chick is fucking out of this world. I can't believe we fell asleep together again. "Baby?" Fuck! I have to quit calling her baby. I remember other things I said during sex and I need to keep my tongue in check. But, what if I don't fucking want to keep my tongue in check. What if I want her to know everything? Just because we have limited time doesn't mean it can't be good and mean something. Listen to me, mean something. Good and meaningful when you have less than three days and there's an end only hours away? Not. "Baby?" Shit! I kiss her cheek. "I'm going to take the steaks out. You hungry?"

She nods at me without opening her eyes.

"You sleep, baby," Fuck! Watch the 'baby' already, "I'll come and get you when the steaks are ready."

"No, don't leave me." She wraps her hand around my arm and doesn't let go.

"I'm not leaving you. I'm cooking dinner, honey." Honey? What the freaking hell?

She doesn't let go and I watch her. She's sleeping. "Robbi, sweetheart?" Damn it all to hell. Baby, honey, and now sweetheart? Fuck me.

She makes a sweet girlie noise and smiles, turning my insides into mush.

"Are you hungry?"

"Yeah."

"Okay, I'm going to cook dinner on the grill. I'll be right outside."

"No, stay."

"I can't cook and stay."

"Take me with."

"Okay, get up, baby," Damn it!

"We can eat later. Hold me and love me, Mick."

Did she say what I think she said? It's what I want and I can't have it. But I can have it for now. Dinner can wait. I hold her tight and watch her sleep. She'll wake up soon, but until then I have permission to hold her and love her—that's all I want to do. I let myself imagine what it would be like to keep Robbi. Everything we could do together. Living together and having her here with me all the time. I can see us getting married and the mere thought makes my body ache because it will never happen. I can never do that to this beautiful woman. She deserves better. She deserves a man who will take care of her and come home to her every night.

It's late in the evening when Robbi wakes up in my arms. I'm holding her tight against me and kissing her forehead. I stayed in bed with her, torn between how much I want to be with her, wondering if this is love and knowing I can't keep her. For now, her body feels incredible next to mine and even if I can't have her, I can keep an eye on her and try to keep her safe.

"Are you ready to get up and grill steak, baby?" Damn it!

"This is nice, just like this," She says and smiles as she gazes up at me.

I kiss her lips sweetly, "Whatever you want."

It's almost midnight when hunger wins and I've had hours to think about dinner. I get up and pull on shorts and a T-shirt. She's watching me with her big eyes and smiling, but making no attempt to get out of bed. "Take your time and meet me on the patio. Dinner should be ready in about forty minutes." I kiss her sweet lips and drag myself away.

I wander through my kitchen, taking the steaks out of the refrigerator, grabbing a bottle of red wine from the bottom of my pantry and looking for an easy yet tasty side dish. I put the wine in the refrigerator to chill. I set the steaks outside by the grill to come to room temperature and get the grill going. I get the old metal baking pan I use on my grill and pour in enough olive oil to make it about a quarter inch deep. I add a spoonful of butter and a package of onion soup mix, stirring it all together. The smell of it makes my stomach rumble and I search for veggies to roast in it. I find a couple of potatoes and slice them up thin, so I have enough time to get them cooked and toss them into the pan. I give the pan a shake to make sure all the pieces are coated and cover it with foil. I put the pan on the grill and close it. I clean up the patio table, wiping down the chairs and the table-top. I get the table set with plates, glasses, silverware, napkins, and wish I had candles because it's so dark, quiet and still—candlelight would be perfect. I glance up and remember the twinkle lights Dino put up. I plug them in and flip the patio light switch off, it's perfect and better than having an open flame. I turn the patio light back on and check the potatoes. Everything is going as planned. I grab the bag of leftover green salad from the refrigerator and chop up a tomato to add to it. I drizzle some olive oil and balsamic vinegar into the bag, then turn to the refrigerator for something else to add. I find a small chunk of Parmesan cheese and shave off slices to add to the bag. I seal the bag with everything in it and shake it until the oil and vinegar are no longer pooled in the bottom of the bag. It's about time to grill the steaks and my girl isn't here yet.

My girl? I look around myself and realize I put together a romantic meal to share with Robbi. What the fuck am I doing? She's not my girl. Fuck it. She can be my girl for tonight and maybe tomorrow. She deserves everything I can give her and more.

Robbi

If I wasn't hungry I wouldn't have let Mick out of bed. There's something about him. He has the magic trifecta—magic kiss, out of my mind sex and fireman hands. I could probably stay in his bed and never leave it, if nature didn't call and my stomach would stop rumbling. Reality can be such a bitch, always ruining something I'm enjoying, maybe want, and reminding me I can't have it. I spend a few minutes in the bathroom getting cleaned up and fixing my hair. I pull on my shorts, bra and tank top, and go to the patio to find Mick. The smell of food makes me hungrier. I get to the kitchen door and lean there out of his sight, watching him as he gets the table ready and tends to the grill. I hide around the other side of the wall when he comes into the kitchen and watch quietly as he puts salad in a bowl and retrieves a bottle of wine from the refrigerator, taking both out to the patio with him. He opens the grill and puts the steaks on. He has a pan of something covered in foil that he pokes at and takes off the grill. I walk out to the patio and wrap my arms around his waist from behind, leaning my head on his back. His hands are busy, but I feel his body relax at my touch. "You didn't need to do all of this."

He closes the grill and turns to me, running his hands down my arms. He smiles, "I want to cook dinner for you. You deserve more." He takes my hand and leads me to the table. He pulls the chair out for me to sit down and pushes me in. He screws the corkscrew into the wine bottle and pulls the cork, pouring a glass for each of us. He opens the grill and his reaction tells me the steaks are perfect. He takes the plates off the table and flips off the patio light.

The night is calm and still. Surrounded by the darkness with only the twinkling lights and the glow of the pool off in the distance. The reflection of the lights shining on the wine glasses draws me in and I'm warm all over. It's romantic and sweet and I can't believe he did any of this. "You really didn't need to go to any trouble for me."

"Do you like it?"

"Yeah."

"Good." He sets down two plates, each with a steak, potatoes and salad.

It looks delicious and I'd eat it all even if I weren't starving.

"My girl deserves everything."

I'm not sure what to think about his "my girl" comments. Should I say something? I guess I'm his girl for now and I should go along with it. I'd love to be his girl, but that's not an option. Fuck. This is going to end badly. Suck it up and enjoy it. Maybe I should tell him how I feel about him? Maybe he deserves me. Stick to your rules, Robbi. You know better.

He sits down across from me, then gets up and moves over to sit next to me. He smiles at me and picks up his wine glass to toast, he stops and hesitates, "To the most beautiful woman I've ever met." His expression says he has more words to say, but he keeps them to himself. Probably best that way, but I want to ask what he held back. We clink glasses and drink. He takes my glass from me and sets them both on the table. He leans in and kisses me long and tender, conveying the rest of his words silently. I kiss him back, needing to respond that I feel the same way. But, we both know we can't stay together. We both have our reasons. He pulls back and whispers, "You're perfect. Don't let anyone ever tell you different." If I'm perfect, tell me you want to break your rules. Tell me you want us to be together. Take a risk and push me to take the risk with you. The sound of my voice in my head sounds like a whiny girl and I want to slap myself.

We sit together and eat dinner, playing footsie under the table. "This is really good."

"Thank you. One thing I can do well is grill a steak."

"You do everything well, at least I haven't found anything you're bad at yet. I can think of a couple things you excel at." I giggle and put my hand on his crotch. He takes my hand off his crotch and holds it while we finish eating. It's silly, but it makes my heart beat faster. I can't remember the last time a man actually wanted to hold my hand.

ELEVEN

Robbi

Mick stands, still holding my hand, "Get your glass." He had his glass in his other hand and the bottle of wine under is wing. He leads me to the hot tub, setting the wine and glasses nearby. He wraps his arms around me, hugging me like he never wants to let go. His hands move to my waist, lifting my top and caressing my skin. He drops to his knees, to kiss me in the same place and stretches up to pull my top off. He reveals my black lace bra pushing my breasts together and stands to appreciate the view. He unbuttons my shorts, "I wonder what I'll find here." He pushes them down and I step out of them, commando. "You're a very bad girl," he says while he pulls his T-shirt off and then takes my bra off. His hands go to my breasts as they're released and his tongue follows exploring my cleavage. I unbutton his board shorts and push them down slowly, leaving us both standing their naked. He gets a dirty glint in his eyes, "Want to sit on my lap and drink wine in the hot tub?"

I simply smile and follow his lead. He presses his lips to mine, sucking me in to one of his magic kisses and the rest of the world fades away. I wrap my arms around his neck and he lifts me up to his level. I wrap my legs around him and he's hard, reaching for my entrance. I move, rubbing against his tip and he groans into my mouth. We move together while we kiss until he's buried completely inside me, needing to feel each other and be together. He holds me tight against him and steps into the hot tub with me wrapped around him. He sits in the hot water with hot air bubbles from the jets blowing all around and my boobs floating in his face. His lips on mine keep us in our own world and I grind against him, feeling him hard inside me. Straddling him in the hot tub, I move on him up and down, over and over, stroking his hard dick with my wet heat. His protective hands are splayed across my back, enjoying me and my motions.

"Slow down, baby. Let's just be together. Take it slow." He hands me my wine and we both gulp down the rest of our glass. "More?"

"Yes, please."

He pours us each another glass, "I think we both need it."

I nod at him and he swirls his glass around. "I'm a lightweight when it comes to wine," I admit.

He laughs, "So, we should down this one like college kids and get you buzzed?"

I laugh, "Race you."

"You're on. One, two, three... go!"

We both down our fresh glass of wine as quick as possible. I finish first and laugh at him still downing his. I know it's not a good idea, but, "One more bartender."

He splits the remainder of the bottle between us.

I look him in the eyes, "Wine can make you do things. It can also make you forget."

He nods, "It can also bring out the truth."

"Yeah, alcohol can definitely loosen your tongue."

"It makes you want to break rules."

"Or, maybe pretend you can break rules while the wine is in control."

We gaze into each other's eyes and down the wine quickly.

I get nosey, "How long have you been a fireman?"

"Twelve years."

"How many years do you put in before you retire?"

"I plan to do twenty, maybe twenty-five. It depends on my rank and what my duties are. I'll do it longer if I move up into a higher rank that keeps me off the frontline, maybe become a trainer or something."

"Have you ever gotten hurt on the job?"

He looks down and takes a deep breath, "Yes."

I focus on him with big eyes, wanting details.

"Burned many times, sometimes worse than others. Singed my mustache once. Broken ribs from a partial building collapse. Sprained my ankle when I had to drop from a second floor window. I've been lucky. Nothing too major."

"What do your duties have to do with how long you'll do your job?"

He smiles at me, "I've seen too much. I'll only be lucky for so long, then my luck will run out. I want to be done before my luck runs out." He turns away, avoiding eye contact, "And... I don't want to be alone forever. When my duties become safer then I can have a woman I can keep. Quit this one-night stand bullshit." He looks into my eyes like he's searching my soul, "Blame it on the wine or whatever. Robbi, I'd keep you. When I call you my girl, it would be the truth and you'd only ever be my girl. I'd take care of you and hold you every night. I'd give you everything and do my best to make every one of your dreams come true."

"It would be easy because I don't allow myself to have dreams."

"Then I would want to make you safe, so you could dream." He leans into my ear, "I want to make you safe, so you can have dreams now. I want to give you everything. I want to make you happy. I've seen your beautiful smile and what your happy is like. It should be a permanent part of you." He pulls away, "I'm sorry. I should've kept that to myself. What I want doesn't matter because I can't have it."

"What you want matters to me. You should have what you want. What are your dreams?"

"This evening I was daydreaming about a beautiful blonde living with me, playing in the pool with her mini me while I listened to their laughter and made dinner at the grill. I've never dreamed about that before. I've never been so happy as I was in the dream."

"Tell me about the mini me."

His smile widened, "She was three or four. She had your features, but my hair and eye color. Her hair was long and pulled back into a ponytail. She was a skinny little thing, but strong and determined. I think you were showing her how to do handstands and somersaults in the pool."

My whole world falls through the floor. My stomach drops. My head spins. I'm surprised I don't pass out right on the spot. I somehow manage to stay calm. "Um, so it really wasn't a beautiful blonde and her mini me. It was me and a mini us." I search his eyes for clarification. "Mick? It wasn't vague, like you want a blonde and a kid?"

"Fuck. The wine was a bad idea. Damn it! I only want you, and yes, it was us and she was damn beautiful, just like you. I can't have that and it's not real and I should've fuckin' kept it to myself."

"Sharing is important. We both need some release." I turn his face to me, so he can't look away, "I want you, too. Please take me to bed and love me, even if it's just for tonight."

He lifts me off of him and sets me on the edge of the hot tub. It's cold and I quickly get a towel to wrap around me. He catches up with me and picks me up, carrying me like a baby in his arms and kissing me. He takes me to his bedroom and loves me without words until daylight.

TWELVE

Mick

I wake up late for the second day in a row with Robbi naked in my arms. I'm happier today than I was yesterday. She's cuddled into me with her arm around me, holding onto me. She makes me happy. There's got to be a better way, but I'm not dwelling on that. I'm spending the day with her. I hold her close until she wakes up. My dream playing through my head on repeat while I watch her sleep, but I'll keep that to myself and stay away from alcohol today. Then again, she did ask me to love her and there's nothing better.

She stretches and buries her face in my arm while she pulls me closer. I roll toward her and pull her against me, wrapping my arms around her. I kiss the top of her head and wait. A few minutes pass and she makes a whiny noise.

"Good morning, baby. Let's get up and you can help me make muffins. We can try your suggestions."

She reaches around me and grabs my ass, "I like your muffins just the way they are." She laughs because she thinks she's funny, and she is. She jumps out of bed quickly and runs for the bathroom shutting the door behind her. I worry it's going to be a repeat of yesterday, but I hear the toilet flush and the water turn on, then off, and the door opens. She wanders out and thumbs through the small stack of clothes she brought with her, pulling on a pair of denim cutoffs and a tank top with skinny straps that look shiny. She looks at me, "Are you getting up?"

She distracts me completely. I get up and repeat what she did, but only pull on my cutoff sweatpants. I don't like to get baking stuff on my clothes and aprons are girly. I grab her around the waist and she squeals when I fireman carry her to the kitchen.

"Do you want breakfast or something before we start the muffins?"

"I want the leftover muffin parts from yesterday."

I smile and get the muffin remains out, along with a glass of milk. She has a bite of each and makes a yummy noise that fills me with satisfaction.

"Which one are we starting with?" She looks to me waiting for a response.

"Anything but mixed berries. I'm not berry prepared and they didn't need any work done on them. I was planning on making banana nut today. I have everything for carrot cream cheese, including extra cream cheese. I'm most intrigued by the idea of adding sour cream to the chocolate chip."

"Chocolate chip it is. My favorite." She smiles and continues, "How are you going to change the recipe? You can't add sour cream without taking something out."

I open the cabinet door where my basic muffin recipe is hanging and review it, "I'm going to switch out the yogurt for sour cream."

"You think that'll work?" She glares at me, trying to throw me off my game.

"Yep. So confident I'm going to make a whole batch, not even going with a test batch."

"Okay big man, show me what you've got." She leans against the counter watching me as I gather my dry ingredients and measure them, dumping the flour, baking powder, baking soda, and salt in a bowl and sifting it together.

"Can you turn the oven on to 375 and grab the muffin pans from that cupboard?" I point to the cabinet with the pans. I mix my sugar, vanilla, oil and eggs together in another bowl with the sour cream, then add it to my dry ingredients. I use my big spatula and get everything combined, lumpy and looking like it needs more attention. I add the chocolate bits and reach for the tins.

"You should add more chocolate, or maybe some banana chunks. Ooooh, maybe you should add chocolate to your banana muffins! Chocolate makes everything better."

"Are you making muffins or are these my muffins?" I'm satisfied with the batter, it's the same thickness as when I use the yogurt.

"Your muffins need more chocolate and I want to squeeze them, too." She steps behind me and grabs my ass, one cheek at a time.

I dump more chocolate pieces into the batter and give it a quick stir to get them distributed through the batter. I walk outside with the muffin tins and hit them with the non-stick spray. I walk back into the kitchen with her eyes focused on me and fill the muffin tins. The oven beeps letting me know it's at the right temperature and I slide the muffins into the oven. I set a timer and turn to Robbi, "Banana nut next and I'll let you add chocolate to part of them."

She claps happily and I start the process for my banana nut muffins. I chop the nuts finer and when I'm about done with the batter, "This is how many nuts I usually add, and you can see I chopped them finer per your suggestion. More nuts?"

"More is better." She takes a big handful of nuts out of the bag and drops them on the counter. It's almost as much as I had in the batter already. I go with it and chop them up fine. I dump them in my batter and stir them in. I spray my tins and start to fill them up, "What about the chocolate."

I roll my eyes, "Don't get your panties in a bunch. I'm only using half the batter and then you can add the chocolate to the other half."

"My panties aren't in a bunch. I'm not wearing any." I can't help but check out her ass in those cutoff jeans to make sure there are no panty-lines. I know better, she goes commando. I found that out first hand, or maybe I should say finger.

"You know what I mean. Everything doesn't have to be about... never mind." Why fight it when I like it?

She giggles like she knows what I'm thinking and takes the bowl of batter away from me. She swipes her finger across the edge of the bowl, giving it a taste, "Mmmm. Add the chocolate."

I grab the bowl back from her and finish the first half, then give her the bag of chocolate and hold the bowl of batter in front of her, "Dump what you want."

She's beautiful, to see her smile you'd think she doesn't have a care in the world. The way her eyes shine at me, makes me want to take care of her and see her like this everyday. Joyful as a child. I stir the overabundance of chocolate into my, no, her banana chocolate chip muffins and fill the tins.

The timer for the chocolate chip muffins goes off and I stop what I'm doing to check on them. They're perfect. I've made them so many times I've got it down to a science. After all, baking is a science. I pull the muffins from the oven and set them upside down on a tea towel. I finish filling her muffin tins, under her close scrutiny. "Did I do okay?"

"It'll do."

I shake my head and slide the muffins into the oven. I set the timer again and turn around to find Robbi sitting on the counter sucking on her finger. "What are you doing? You know that has raw eggs."

She looks at me defiantly and keeps sucking on her finger, then swiping it across the bowl and licking it clean. I don't remember ever getting a hard-on from making muffins before. She sticks her finger out to me, "Want a taste?" Yes, but not of the batter. Fuck me. I walk over to her and suck her finger into my mouth. I press my lips to hers and grasp her hips. I'm tempted to take her right on my counter, but in my head I want her to know she's more.

I pick her up and hold her to me, breaking the kiss and I whisper in her ear, "You're so beautiful and funny. You really are perfect. You make everything better, just like more nuts and too much chocolate in everything." I kiss her below her ear and give her tasty neck a nibble before I set her back down on the counter and get ready to move on to the carrot cream cheese muffins.

I flip the chocolate chip muffins over and set them upright on the cooling rack. I grab one and cut it into chunks on the counter next to Robbi. You can see the heat escaping and the smell of the chocolate has Robbi breathing deep. We each take a piece and give it a taste. She takes another and another and another. "Does that mean you approve?"

"It's chocolate." She says with her mouth full. "It's better, what do you think?"

"If you say it's better, that's all that matters." I can't help myself when I look at her, she's my everything. I wrap my arms around her and kiss her because having her next to me makes my heart beat stronger and my eyes see clearer. I'm in trouble here, completely out of my comfort zone, and consider breaking the rules, but it would be for the wrong reason. It's not fair to her.

She doesn't deserve to worry over me. I'll have to deal with it. Protecting her is the right thing to do. However, the thought doesn't keep me from wanting to have her right on the counter. I control myself and make out with her until the banana nut muffins are ready to come out of the oven, then I carry her away to my bedroom for extracurricular activities.

THIRTEEN

Robbi

I'm not sure what happened. I open my eyes and Mick says, "You should nap, baby. I'm going to finish the muffins." He kisses my cheek and beams at me with his gorgeous blue eyes as he walks out of the room. I'm naked and content in his bed. I'm relaxed and a nap sounds nice. I remember him picking me up off his counter and taking me to his room. Memories flash through my mind of him kissing me, touching me, needing me, fucking me. Both of us completely out of control. Everything just disappeared and he took me away. He's truly amazing and you aren't going to believe this, but I mean in ways other than sex. Well, definitely an A+ in sex with an O for Outstanding Effort and a five out of five for Participation. I won't take that away from the man. Just the way he touches me makes me feel like I'm more and deserve better. Add his cooking skills and willingness to make his muffins better. He says I'm perfect, but he must be looking in a mirror and not at me.

I close me eyes and drift off, finding myself in a dream. I'm watching previews, but it's not movies—it's my life. I see us sitting in a nice restaurant together sharing desert while he holds my hand. I see us camping out somewhere and spending the night together sleeping (and not sleeping) in the back of his truck. I see us sitting in his kitchen eating dinner together and all the meals that he makes for us. I see him looking at me happily while I marvel at a diamond ring on my left ring finger. I see us sitting on his couch and watching hockey together. I see us sharing a lounger at his pool together. I see me waking up day after day in his bed to him telling me how much he loves me. I see me happy.

Robbi

"Robbi, you hungry? I don't want to wake you, but I made dinner. It's nothing special, I was getting hungry and thought you'd be hungry, too." I smile knowing it's going to be delicious and pull his T-shirt on. He takes my hand and kisses my forehead, "Always so beautiful, even in my boring old T-shirt." He leads me to the kitchen and we sit at his counter together eating pasta covered in a spicy Italian sausage meat sauce with tomatoes. I'm hit with deja vu when he reaches for my hand while we're eating and put my fork down to gather control.

"Is the pasta okay?" He asks, probably because I stopped eating.

"It's delicious. I love the spicy sauce."

He stops and looks at me straight on. "What's wrong?"

"Deja vu." Oh, and I don't have dreams, but I did today when I was in your bed.

"We didn't have this meal before."

"I was dreaming this afternoon and we had it then."

He smiles, "Dreams? Anything interesting?"

"Not really," Not wanting to give up anything because one of them is already coming true and I know the others won't happen.

They can't happen. Not possible. I get lucky and he doesn't press the subject. We finish dinner and all I want is him. I want to show him how I... well, I want to make sure he can't forget me. We leave our dishes sitting on the counter and spend the night together in bed, both of us fully aware it's the last night and not talking about it, not wanting to think about it or acknowledge the truth.

Mick's hands are on me, touching me lightly and caressing my skin and curves like he's trying to memorize the shape and feel of my body. His lips soft and cherishing everywhere they touch. His kiss claims me as his. Nothing about the night was just sex. The night was everything. His sweet words in my ear. His insatiable desire for me. His tender movements. He said everything he could that means he loves me without saying he loves me, and I did the same.

Mick

I want to hold her forever and tell her I love her, but it makes no sense. We've only known each other for almost three days and besides, I can't keep her. We made our rules, nobody made them for us. At least I have tonight and tomorrow morning. I need to come up with a reason to see her on a regular basis, even if it's not romantically. I can still watch out for her and make sure she's okay. I need to get her phone number, too. If nothing else we're friends and she can hang out and watch the game with the crew and I. Or not, I don't want her hooking up with one of my crew. Damn it. I can't control what she does and who she does it with. I want it to only be me. I need to make sure nobody compares to me. My goal tonight is to show her how I feel and prove nobody is worthy of her, except maybe me.

Robbi

The sex the last three days has been the best I've ever had, but now it's 3am and our three days is up in the morning. Mick is out for the night with a smile plastered on his face that will probably be there for days. My smile matched his until I found myself awake by myself in this quiet time. It's time to go. He would give me a ride home tomorrow, but I don't want the scene. I definitely don't want anyone to know I care, and the truth is I fell for Mick. I don't want to leave him, and I refuse to be that woman who puts him in the position of physically and mentally walking away from me. We both knew the rules and I love to defy authority, truly believe rules are meant to be broken. This is different, I know what I signed up for—three amazing days of fireman observation with off the charts sex. And let me tell you, I got it.

I carefully slide out of bed and gather all of my things up into my arms on my way to disappear into the bathroom. I get ready to go and make sure I have everything in my bag. I already have silent tears running down my face, so I move quickly to avoid any possible sobbing. I get my lipstick from my bag and write on his bathroom mirror:

Mick,

You're the best I've ever had, and that's saying something when it comes from me. Thought it best to leave now. No expectations. Clean break.

<3
Robbi

I grab the box of tissues from his bathroom and take his station T-shirt with me. I sneak out the back door and text Carlos to pick me up, hoping he's still working. Carlos is my personal driver, well he was the Uber guy that almost always came to get me and I got his number, so now it's always him.

"Hey Robbi, what are you doing way out here? There's no bars here." He unlocks the door for me.

I hop in the backseat. "What are you still doing out picking people up? Isn't it too late for the bar closing crowd?"

"You'd be surprised. They hang on at a couple of places and midweek like this there aren't many drivers out, so I end up going back and forth a lot." He glances at me in his rearview mirror and I know I'm tear-stained, even if I'm doing a hell of a job holding back the sobs. "You okay?"

"Yep."

"Not being mean, but you don't look it. Did somebody hurt you? We should call the police." He starts to pull over.

"No. Nobody hurt me. He would never physically hurt me."

"If you're sure." He gets back to the middle of the highway. "I haven't seen you in a few days. What have you been doing?"

I smirk to myself, "Breaking the rules."

"Just like you." He pulls up in front of my place and doesn't pry.

I hand over my money, "Thanks." I turn and walk the twenty steps home, locking the door behind me, and everyone out of my life.

FOURTEEN

Robbi

It's been almost a week and I've only left home to go to work. Mostly I'm wallowing and mad at myself. I know better. Why would he call? I didn't give him my number. Neither one of us do second dates. He's the hottest man ever and he's a fireman. I guess, I don't know, maybe I thought there was more between us. I swear he said things that meant more when he was whispering in my ear, and I could've been misinterpreting his eyes. On top of that, my tips have sucked this week because... Fuck! I'm heartbroken. I miss him so much it hurts and I don't want anybody else. My cheeks are chapped from tears. I haven't been crazy, outgoing and forward. You know it's bad when Carlos texts me to see if I'm okay or need a ride. The drive-thru dairy guy already has the ice cream flavor I want ready for me when I drive up, not a good precedent, and I haven't eaten anything other than ice cream and potato chips since I left Mick's.

I need to pull myself out of this funk and get on with it. Honestly, put on my big girl pants, but I just don't feel like it.

Mick

Dino walks into the workout room at the station, "Seven Nation Army" by The White Stripes is blaring loud. He turns down the volume and stands in front of me while I lift weights on the bench. "Captain, I've been watching you and I think something's bothering you."

"Thanks for the observation. Go away. Turn the music back up on your way out."

"You've been in here hiding from the crew for hours everyday and on your days off you swim lap after lap at home in your pool. It's been weeks and the only thing that's changed is the music. Yesterday was AC/DC, day before was Alice in Chains, I remember hearing Metallica and Breaking Benjamin last week."

"Get lost," I bark.

"Do you want me to tell you what I think?"

"No, I want you to go away."

"You should call her."

"I didn't ask for your opinion," but it sounded more like get the fuck out and leave me alone.

"The crew is tired of getting barked at, you need to do something."

"I don't have her number and even if I did, I wouldn't call her."

"You thinking you should just go to her place? That's probably a better plan," Dino pushes for a positive spin.

"No, I'm thinking I should forget about her and if I lift enough, work hard enough, maybe it will all go away."

"I don't understand. She's perfect. Why do you want her to go away? I understand why she left after the three days, the time was up and she didn't want to make any assumptions. I would've called her as soon as I knew she was gone."

I remember waking up alone in my bed. It had only been a few days, but my bed was empty without her. I called out her name, hoping she would answer and thinking she might be in the kitchen making breakfast or something. I got out of bed and searched around the house, checking the pool and everywhere—no sign of Robbi. I looked around my room and her things were gone. I walked into my bathroom to pee and found her lipstick scribble on my mirror. I wish I could say the part about being the best she ever had is what sticks with me, but the words repeating over and over in my head are "No expectations. Clean break." Her note is still on my mirror, but starting to smudge from the shower humidity. I probably shouldn't admit that. She left a handprint on my mirror and I've kissed it like it was her palm every night I'm home in my own bed. I remember her smooth skin and her pouty lips. I can taste her sweetness on my tongue and imagine her wrapped around me. I can hear her cries of pleasure, her sexy whimpers, and her begging for more from me. I miss touching her and kissing her. Most of all, I miss snuggling with her in my recliner, cooking together, swimming together, anything together.

"Captain? You okay? You kinda zoned out there."

"None of it matters. It's over." Why does he have to make me remember her?

"Why does it have to be over? Did you dump her or am I missing something?"

"You know I don't do second dates. She made it clear that she doesn't either. We had the three days and it's over."

"So, you wouldn't break your no second date rule for her? Because I saw the way you two looked at each other and you can make excuses, deny it all you want, it's not going to make it go away."

"I'm not a young dumb hot fireman anymore. You guys can go out and get laid every night, no worries and move onto the next one. I don't want that anymore. I want someone special and I can't have someone special."

"Why not?"

"I don't want the woman I love to be worried about me all the time and wondering if I'm dead somewhere or if a burning building collapsed on me or if the reason my mustache is gone is because it burnt off."

"That's stupid."

"Excuse me?"

"You heard me. You'd rather be miserable for the rest of your life and have her be with somebody else that won't make her near as happy as you do. If you're so worried about it, change duties or resign or do something because we're all tired of the barking." He turns to leave and throws another comment back at me, "Oh, and your muffins sucked this week."

"Damn it!"

Mick - Am I stupid?

Dr PITA - Yes

Dr PITA - Why are you asking now?

Mick - Do you worry about me when I'm at work?

Dr PITA - You know I'm a Dr right?

Dr PITA - I worry about you sometimes, but usually I don't have time to worry about you.

Mick - Would you date a fireman?

Dr PITA - OMG Yes… Are you offering up one of your crew? Which one?

Mick - Keep your panties on.

Mick - I'm not offering up my crew.

Mick - Would you get serious with a fireman?

Dr PITA - Getting serious with a man has nothing to do with what he does.

Dr PITA - We can't control who we love.

Dr PITA - Having said that, I would never be with a bad person.

Dr PITA - No thieves, murderers, etc. I doubt I could love someone like that.

Mick - So, you'd marry a fireman knowing he was running into burning buildings and shit?

Mick - Wouldn't it freak you out? Too much worry?

Dr PITA - I'm sure it would some days.

Dr PITA - Gotta live your life big brother.

Dr PITA - Nobody wants to be tucked away safe in a bubble.

Dr PITA - A little worry in exchange for a lifetime full of happiness with the one I love, doesn't sound like a bad deal to me.

Dr PITA - Who are you setting me up with?

Mick - Shit

Dr PITA - Come on! I want some fireman fun!

Mick - I'll tell you the next time the guys are coming over. You can come, too. Wear a bikini.

Dr PITA - I'll take it!

Dr PITA - How about Dino? He's kinda cute.

Mick - He's a kid.

Dr PITA - You think I'm a kid

Mick - True… Want me to post a note on the bulletin board? Captain's sister wants to date a fireman, call…

Dr PITA - Shut Up!

Mick - Is that a no?

Dr PITA - That's a yes, please! Ha ha!

I'm starting to think I should be worried about my sister. She's smart, but is every woman fireman crazy? It doesn't matter, I'm not going to make the woman I love worry and probably a young widow.

FIFTEEN

Mick

I wake up to someone banging on my door and look around my dark bedroom, not wanting to get out of bed. It's almost 11am. I'm not getting up to answer the door. I don't care who it is. I roll over and attempt to go back to sleep. When I'm sleeping I don't miss her, I'm simply incoherent. Sometimes she's with me in my dreams and I don't want to wake up. Today, I want to sleep and pretend she's here with me. There's still knocking at my door, whoever it is needs to go away. It's my day off and I can stay in bed if I want to. I block it out and go back to sleep.

"What are you doing in bed in the middle of the day?" My sister, Miranda, smacks me with something repeatedly. "You didn't respond to my texts. You didn't answer your door. At least you still leave your back door unlocked." I recognize her fast speech pattern and irritated tone. It reminds me of our mom when we're in trouble, or I guess when I'm in trouble because Miranda has always been perfect.

I wish I could ignore her and she'd go away, but I know my sister and she wouldn't be a successful doctor if she gave up.

She continues to smack me through the blankets, "Get up! I can see you breathing."

I pull the blankets up over my head.

"I'm calling mom in five, four, three, two..."

I sit up and stare at her in time to see her flip-flop aimed at me, "What do you want?"

"What's wrong with you? You need to snap out of this."

"I want to stay in bed. It's my day off and I can do whatever I want."

"You want to mope in bed, wasting your day? Why aren't you swimming or baking muffins?"

"I don't have to explain myself."

"You may be older than me, but I'm not a kid anymore and I'm not stupid. Do you want to know what I think?"

"No."

"Fine, then you get my professional opinion. It's not healthy for you to lie in bed all day in the dark. You've never sat still unless there's a game on."

"There's nothing wrong with me. I work hard and I'm entitled to rest."

"It's my day off, too. Get up and take me to lunch." She wanders into my bathroom to wash her hands and stops when she looks at the mirror. "Mick..." Her tone changes to consoling.

"Fuck. You're not supposed to go in my bathroom." She's looking at the smudged note Robbi left on my mirror in lipstick. Worse, she can probably see my lips on the handprint she left behind. It's the part of her I have left.

"You miss her?"

I cover my head with my own pillow, wishing I could suffocate myself to get out of this conversation.

"Spit it out already."

"It doesn't matter."

She sits down on the edge of my bed and turns to me, speaking softly. "Tell me about her. I liked her when I met her, but I don't know much about her. I know she's self-sufficient and doesn't have much of a support system. She seemed fun and was obviously interested in you."

"She's beautiful inside and out. She's a feisty smart ass. She showed me how my life could be. Seeing her happy, is like the sun shining bright and warm. She gives me the adrenaline rush I get when I run into a burning building. There's nobody else like her. My whole house is alive when she's in it. Fuck! My comfy chair is more comfortable with her in my lap. My bed was always warm and inviting, now it's cold and empty. The whole house is empty."

I get up, grabbing some clothes to change into and walk into my bathroom, closing the door behind me most of the way. "Give me a minute and I'll take you to lunch."

"Does she know you miss her?"

"It doesn't matter. She doesn't do second dates, same as me. It's done."

"By the look of your mirror, I don't think it's done."

"Trust me, it's done. She left in the middle of the night while I was sleeping."

"Did you tell her you wanted her to stay?"

"Why would I do that?"

"Maybe because you're in love with her, you idiot!"

I know she's right, but I haven't admitted it to anyone other than myself and even then I didn't say the words out loud. "You know how I feel about having a woman. I'm married to my job. I'm a fireman first."

"Maybe you need to get a divorce and try making fireman your occupation instead of your life."

"That won't make a difference, I'll still be doing the same

dangerous job." I shake my head. "The fact that I love her isn't enough to make her worry over me and potentially a young widow with a family."

"You need to suck it up and go for it, or change jobs. What's she worth to you? Have you asked her what she wants?"

"I told you, we only do one-night stands."

"Did you say you wanted more? Did you ask her to break the rules with you?"

"No, I respected the rules."

"And, she left because she knew the timer was going to expire." She takes a deep breath, "You need to tell her what you want and stop worrying about the consequences. You are a pretty great guy. I think you would be worth it. You love her, take the risk."

Robbi

It's been almost a month since I left Mick's and today is hair day, yep four weeks since the wet T-shirt incident in the dog grooming tub. I walk into the salon to find Deanna and her expression changes when she looks at me. She gestures for me to sit in her chair, "What's wrong?"

"Nothing. It's hair day and I'm here so you can make me stay blonde."

"Try again. You've never walked into this salon with your hair looking like it hasn't been brushed in days, no make-up at all, you look tired, and your smile is missing."

Shit. I've gotten pretty good at my fake smile at work, my tips have been back to normal. I guess I need to work on keeping it all the time.

"Spill it. Or, maybe we should talk about the hot fireman? He should cheer you up."

I spilled alright, tears everywhere. I couldn't help it.

Deanna dragged me into a private massage room and locked the door. "I've never seen you cry. What happened?"

I tell her everything and it's a relief to get it out.

"Why don't you call him?"

"I don't have his number and I don't want to be a needy girl."

"Just call 911."

"That's even worse."

"Maybe we should set you up a date."

"I don't want to go out with anyone else." I hear the words from my mouth and I can't believe them.

"Did you just say..."

"Shut up. I heard it, too."

Deanna focused on my hair and made it beautiful. I left to go on with my day, without any embarrassing dog groomer incidents, so I count that as a win.

SIXTEEN

Robbi

I'm on the happy hour shift at the bar today and a group of young professionals walk in. A brunette dressed in a pencil skirt and stilettos talking at a million miles a minute is rambling on and on about this fireman that rescued her. Her voice is annoying and high pitched as she continues on about how they fell in love instantly. I admire her rack and wonder if she got her claws into Dino. But, she continues on telling her co-workers how he's older than her and has gorgeous clear blue eyes.

She has my attention now. The more she says, the more it sounds like Mick. There's no way it's Mick, he only does one-night stands. It must be me being oversensitive. I left him in his sleep, but it still hurt. It never hurts to leave a man. Mick? He's different. I think about him every day. I search for him every time I hear an emergency vehicle. I haven't been with another man since I met him, and I don't want to. I'm simply not interested in anyone else. I've always blown off guys that want a second date and he knows it. I miss him and I wish he'd come after me. I wish he missed me. I want to see him. I've even thought about driving by the station to see if I could catch a glimpse of him, but what's the point? I'm not going to park and walk in to find him. We both knew the rules. We live by the same rules. It's why he's perfect. Three days we were done. Turns out, it's not the best rule when it comes to us. There's no way he's interested in this girl with the perfect hair and the nice rack. Who am I kidding? He must be back to his routine of one-night stands. Why wouldn't he be interested in her? She's probably a size six and doesn't have an ounce of fat on her. But, that voice! Who would want to listen to it? She's too uptight for him. She won't do the things he wants and needs, she probably doesn't know how. It can't be Mick.

I hover close, listening while I tend to the neighboring tables and I hear her say, "He's so handsome! I was going to make muffins for him since that's his name, but I baked cookies instead. It wasn't a good day for him though. He was busy, so I'm going back to see him tomorrow when he has more time."

No fucking way. I mean, whatever. He's not mine. He can date whoever he wants. It's not like I care. He let me walk and didn't look for me. Why would he when he has a never ending stream of women that he rescues? Was I a notch in his bedpost? Nobody special, simply another hole to fuck? It didn't feel that way. His whispers were so much more. I don't think he's that smooth, but I only spent three days with him.

I was irritated my whole shift. Hurt really. I know I shouldn't be. Mick is just another guy. Another one-night stand, no different than all of the rest. I can't sleep and when I finally fall asleep, I dream about him. I see his dream of me and our mini me. I try to ignore it.

I wake up the next morning thinking about him and drive by the station. Nobody will notice me or think anything of it if they do. I'm driving through town. Nothing out of the ordinary. The station looks quiet, no action or movement around it at all. I hit the grocery store and get some lunch. I drive back by the station and this time Mick is out in front with the brunette from the bar. This can't be happening! I slow down. I make a u-turn and take a second pass, just to make sure I'm seeing what I'm seeing. He's leaned over her with his hands on her car boxing her in. I can see the heat in his eyes, he's red with desire and he's in her face.

I'm torn and tears flow down my cheeks. I want to pull over and remind him who I am, show him that he wants me and not her. Ask him if he wants to be together. I sob at the mere idea because I want it, but I know my place and leave. I stop at the drive-thru dairy for ice cream and hide at home eating the whole pint.

Mick

"Muffin, she's here again." The rookie pokes his head into my office.

"Get rid of her." This is some crazy broad.

"Uh, she's right here."

Fuckin' rookies can't handle business.

This is the third time this week Ms. Prissy has shown up at the station looking for me.

Serves me right for going beyond the call last weekend and checking out something that looked suspicious.

I was on duty for the weekend. You never know what's going to happen on a Friday or Saturday night. A car had caught on fire out on the edge of town and the call came in as a possible rescue mission, two people in the vehicle. Standard procedure. Hope the people got out of the vehicle, get there as quickly as possible and extinguish the fire. No problem, other than the fire started while they were in the backseat naked together. We got them a couple of blankets, so they could cover up. Put out the fire and called someone to pick them up. The vehicle would have to go through an investigation to determine the cause of fire, but tonight it would be towed to the impound lot for storage.

It was on the way back to the station when the night took an odd turn. A light was flashing on the hillside below an office building. Nothing any of my crew or I had ever seen before. We reported in and instead of going back to the station, we took a detour to investigate the flashing light. We watched the light flash, three times in a row and then stop, repeatedly and not with any set timing. We pulled into the parking lot of the office building and scanned the hillside not sure what we were going to find. I suspected teenagers partying, which could be a problem if they were smoking. The hillsides are dry and waiting for the right moment to combust.

"Oh fudge!" I hear come from the hillside. The feminine voice continued, "No, no, no! Where are you?"

I watched quietly from a distance and realized the light flashing three times in a row was her phone when a text message came in. What I don't understand is why she didn't use her phone to call for help. She's a young woman, I'd guess mid-twenties and she's dressed in a skirt and jacket with high heels. She's standing on a small, uneven dirt ledge and holding onto a branch growing out the side of the hillside for security.

"Miss, stay right there and we'll get you back up to the parking lot in no time." I call down to her. Unfortunately, I startled her and she slipped. She dug her heels in for traction and her pointy stiletto heels found a weak spot, causing chunks of dirt to fall from under her feet. She screamed and clung to the branch she was holding. It made sense to hold on, but everything she did was hurting her cause. The pull she was putting on the branch was loosening it and I could see the events transpiring quickly. We didn't have time to wait for anyone else to get there, she would end up farther down the hillside and possibly injured. "Are you okay?"

"Does scared count? I'm afraid of heights."

"No problem. Don't look down. We'll get you to safety and quick as we can. No injuries?"

"A couple of scrapes is all."

I quickly put on a harness and attach a line to the truck as my base, knowing I don't need it because the ledge is only about 5 feet down. I climb down to the ledge and lift her up to my crew in the parking lot. Easy rescue and I climbed back up to stable ground on my own. No injuries to speak of, but when I got to the parking lot and removed the harness—she attacked me.

"Thank you so much for saving me. I would've died on that ledge for sure! Nobody would help me. I'd called all my friends and co-workers. I was left there and forgotten."

"Did you try calling 911?"

"Oh, no." She looked at me with those eyes I've seen before and grabbed onto me. I hoped I was wrong, but she had all the signs of Savior Syndrome. "Thank you for saving me. You saved my life."

"It's my job. No problem." My crew peeled her off of me as I hastily tried to get back to the truck. The EMT's took over, examining her and we returned to the station.

She has shown up at the station looking for me everyday since. The first day I wasn't here. The second day I made the mistake of talking to her and she came back a couple hours later with fresh baked cookies and a picnic basket, wanting me to go on a picnic with her. I told her I couldn't leave the station, that we always eat together. She accepted my response and sat in her car crying for hours before she finally left. She's been by a couple other times, but I've been able to duck out to avoid her.

I don't want the drama and I'm not interested in women. I'm still trying to get over Robbi, but I don't think I ever will—I don't want to get over her.

Now, she's here again and I can't avoid her. Whichever one of my crew members let her in is going to hear about this. I've got some extra duties lined up just for them.

"There you are! I'm so sorry about the picnic. I should know better than to assume you can leave work whenever you want to. Of course you can't! You have such an important job. I'm so sorry to put you in the position of having to choose me or saving people that are in danger. You are basically a superhero." She unbuttons her top two buttons and adjusts her push up bra to accentuate her breasts. She lets her hair down and gives it a shake. I'm not interested.

"I appreciate that, but I have my duties to tend to."

"Oh, I get it. You want to come over to my place later? The privacy would be better. Smart move."

"No, I'm not going to your place. Thank you. You take care of yourself now." I turn to walk away and she flips the fuck out.

"You can't just walk away from me!"

I need to get her out of the station. I walk outside and she follows me. When she is right behind me, I turn on her, "Get in your car and go home."

"I saw the look in your eyes when you rescued me, risking your life for me. You'd do anything for me. I know we belong together. You're amazing. We can get together when you are off work."

"We are never getting together. Go home."

She steps toward me and reaches her arms around my neck, gazing into my eyes. She puckers her lips, angles her mouth toward mine and closes her eyes, waiting for me to kiss her. She's a nut case. I back her up to her car and lean in close, my hands planted on her car around her. I'm loud and heated, "Go the fuck home. I'm not interested in you. Rescuing people is my job. I got paid to rescue you and I would've done the same thing for anyone. Do you understand me?" I stare into her eyes waiting for her to respond.

"I understand. You are scared of what you are feeling for me. I know it's confusing. It can take time." She smiles at me happily and flutters her eyelashes.

"No." My voice is mean and the heat on my face tells me I'm red, "I'm not interested. I'm a one woman man and you are not her." I smack the roof of her car at the realization and turn walking away from the crazy woman with visions of Robbi naked in my bed.

Robbi

I go to work focused on tips and flirting extra to earn good ones. I need to get him out of my head. If he is back to dating, I should be too. I don't need a man, I just like to play with them.

I'm working the happy hour shift again and the brunette walks in with a couple girls. Her friends hanging on her closely, I get nosey to see if I can hear anything about Mick.

Her tall friend that resembles a horse reasons with her, "He's too old for you anyway. You don't want a firefighter. You'll never know if he'll survive through the day. It will be a worry for you every time he leaves for work and I know you don't want worry lines."

She's upset and bawling in public. I want to go to her. I know what it's like to be hooked on Mick. I'm about to tell her he only does one-night stands, if he dates at all, when her model-like blonde friend opens her mouth.

She's ditzy with long legs and constantly giggling, "You still have your boyfriend. You weren't going to dump him for the fireman anyway."

I want to punch her! She doesn't deserve him for anything.

SEVENTEEN

Mick

It's been almost two months and I can't get Robbi out of my head. I want to know she's okay. I need to see her. I want to look in her eyes to see if she needs me, too.

Dino sticks his head in my office, "I'm going to schedule the two month inspection on the potential water heater explosion at the salon. Are you in on that crew since you were on the original crew for the call?"

"Why would it be any different for this inspection than it is for any other?"

"Just making sure."

"Hey, do you think you can schedule it for when Robbi's there? I'd just like to see her and know she's okay. A glance when I'm walking through the salon, you know?"

"I already did that, Muffin Man." He grins at me, knowingly.

"Dino, I know I always say you're a kid. How old are you and are you single?"

"I'm flattered, Captain, but you're not my type." He laughs, "I don't look my age, but I'm 30 and I'm single."

"Have you met my sister?"

"Yes sir, I've met Dr. Muffin. Intelligent woman, seems like quite the handful."

"Interested in dating her?"

"Date a gorgeous doctor? Hell, yes."

"I'll set it up and get her your number. She wants to date a fireman. I told her she's crazy."

"Thanks." Dino turns and gets back to work.

Mick - You have a date with Dino

Mick - He's not as young as he looks

Mick - Sending you his contact info, he's expecting you to contact him

Dr PITA - Are you kidding me?

Mick - He said you're gorgeous and intelligent

Dr PITA - I'm in love already

Mick - Kill me now

Dr PITA - Thanks, Bro!

Maybe I should ask Robbi out when I see her. I could take her some flowers. She'll think I'm crazy because she doesn't go on second dates. Just go on the inspection and see what happens.

Robbi

It's been almost two months and I'm still not dating. I close my eyes at night and I still see, feel, smell, taste, and want Mick. It's never been like this. It's always been hit it and quit it. I know, I can be such a guy. But, it served me well until Mick. I wouldn't change a thing about the way I've lived my life. I've had fun, probably more than my share. It seems he makes me want something else. The fun doesn't interest me anymore. I want to see him and know if he's okay. I want to know if he misses me and thinks about me, like I think about him. I've driven by the station when I'm out doing errands and look to see if I can see him, but I never do. I've thought about going by his house to visit, but I don't know if I'd be welcome. For all I know, he's pissed at me for leaving in the middle of the night. He's made no contact with me, not even attempted any contact with me that I know of.

I'm thinking about him more today because it's hair day again. I pull on my denim short shorts and plain white V-neck T-shirt, and slip into my flip-flops on my way to the salon. Deanna had called to confirm with me and we made a lunch date for after our appointment. I wander into the salon to find Deanna.

"Hi, you still look like you aren't sleeping well. Back out dating?" Deanna tries to make small talk.

"No. I might be over it."

She looks at me in the mirror, "You? Quit dating?"

"I don't know. I guess maybe. Honest, I can't stop thinking about Mick." I release a deep breath at the admission.

"Happens to the best of us sooner or later."

"I probably won't see him again though. I'm not going to go looking for him. If he wanted me, he'd find me. He knows where I live. I'm not going to force myself on him. He needs to want me... Right?" I look to Deanna for her opinion.

"In an ideal world, yes. Sometimes guys need to know you're interested. You two kind of set a time limit and then you enforced it, you don't know if he still wanted you to leave. He could feel like you left him."

"Because I did." I stop and realize how I chose my pride over the possibilities by leaving early while he was asleep. I'm wishing I'd given the possibilities a chance. "What should I do? Write him a letter? Send him an invitation to dinner? Show up at his place naked?"

"Let's think about it and talk about it over lunch." She looks at me in the mirror and doesn't say anything about how I'm still not taking care of myself, but I can see that she notices. "The nail girl had a cancelation, so I'm going to have her do your nails while I do your hair. I think you need a special treat." She smiles at me, helping me get my act back together. "It's been two months."

My fingernails get painted a translucent opalescent pink called See-Thru My Heart and Deanna takes extra time with my hair, doing an extra conditioning treatment and styling it all soft and fluffy. Just as she finishes and takes the smock off of me, there's a commotion around the salon. Everyone is primping and then I see Dino walk in with a clipboard on his way toward the water heater.

I look to Deanna, "That's weird."

"They're doing a two month inspection to make sure there are no more issues."

I see salt and pepper hair follow after Dino, and my heart races at the thought of Mick being here. I turn to Deanna and look at her questioningly, like she would know if he was here. Her smile grows as I'm looking at her and she's looking at something behind me.

I turn quickly and there he is, standing focused on me from about eight feet away. Mick, wearing black dickies and his black fitted button up uniform shirt, looking professional and better than I remember. My heart beats harder simply being in his presence.

I glare at him teasing, "What are you looking at?" Smiling from ear to ear because I can't help it, I can't even keep up the glare for ten seconds.

"The most beautiful girl in the world." I giggle and feel myself blush. "You like breaking rules?"

"You know I do."

"Break the no second dates rule with me and go out with me. We never went on a date. Let me take you out, Robbi."

"Just one, because we don't do second or third dates?" I ask tentatively.

"Rules are made to be broken. I miss you. I don't want a time limit. I want you. No rules." He searches my eyes and I don't know how to answer.

"I'm sorry I left early. I thought it would make it easier on both of us to not have to worry about saying goodbye."

"Do you want to date a fireman?"

"Only if it's you."

"Is it going to be too much for you? I don't want you to worry about me while I'm at work."

"There's no way worrying about you can be worse than being without you."

He moves in close and holds me, whispering in my ear, "I'm done with stupid rules. All I've been able to do for the last two months is think about you." He kisses me there below my ear and continues, "I can't be without you any longer. I want you watching TV in my recliner with me, and in my bed every night. My house feels empty without you."

I reach my arms up around his neck and jump up wrapping my legs around him. He catches me and holds me against him. He's harder and more muscular, my hands travel his shoulders and back, exploring. "No more rules. Maybe one."

"What's that?"

"It's only me and you."

"I like that rule."

Dino stops in his tracks as he's walking back by, "That's much better." He smiles and sends an air five toward me, when I hear Deanna laugh and realize it was a set up.

"Did Deanna just air five?" I ask Mick.

"Yeah."

"We were set up."

He pulls back and gazes at my face, "I don't even care. It got you back in my arms." His heart is beating strong and fast, and there's a shake to his breath, "I love you, Robbi."

I don't question his words and I've questioned those three words every time any other man has said them to me. I've never repeated them back or said them at all. The sincerity in is eyes pull them from me, "I love you, Mick." Saying the words that I've felt for months now is freeing and I'm warm all over. I've been freed. He saved me from the rest of the world and my past. I don't want to be saved from him.

EPILOGUE

Robbi

I've been at Mick's house every night he's home. He meant it when he said he wanted me in his bed every night. He doesn't like my late work schedule at the bar. He's dragged part of his crew to the bar with him to hang out. It was obvious he wanted to check it out and make sure I was safe or maybe be there to defend me if I had trouble with male patrons. He doesn't approve of the low cut and snug fitting T-shirt I'm required to wear for work or the tight jeans I choose to wear with it, and I've explained the concept of tips to him multiple times. He understands, but doesn't like it. He also thinks I could find a different job or maybe switch to the day shift. When I get to his place at about 3am on his off days, he sleeping. We have a routine. He goes to bed early and when I climb into bed with him, I'm his for hours until I fall asleep in his arms. He wakes up earlier than me and does stuff around his house, then makes us breakfast. He always gives me a couple hours more to sleep, sometimes crawling back in bed with me to hold me.

Tonight as I walk around to the back of his house, the twinkle lights are on and the patio table is set for a romantic dinner. He's got something cooking on the grill and it smells delicious. He meets me at the door and wraps his arms around me, kissing me with an electricity that only comes from him. He takes my hand and twirls me around as he leads me back to the table.

I sit down and gaze at his handsome face, "What's the occasion?"

He smiles broadly and takes both of my hands in his, "Please move in with me."

I start to think about it, but, "Yes. I'd love that."

He hands me a small box, "I know we don't use the front door, but here's your key to it."

I smile at the gesture and wonder what it'll be like to live with him. I'm here half the time anyway, but being here all the time, even when he's at the station will be new for me.

He's happy to have me here with him and I never believed I'd be in this place with a man. Completely trusting anyone is a new experience for me, having Mick is unprecedented.

I lean over to him and kiss him, moving to sit in his lap. His arms wrap around me tight, holding me to him and showing me I'm his. His soft warm lips claiming me to the depths of my soul. He kisses me repeatedly, greedy and open-mouthed. He stands and takes me to our bedroom without eating dinner.

"When I remember what it was like without you... I need to be with you. You make everything better." He lays me down on the bed and I toe my shoes off while he kisses me. His hands slide up my shirt caressing my smooth skin and he pulls my shirt off. He leaves a line of warm kisses on my collarbone as he unhooks my bra and tosses it across the room. He focuses his mouth on my neck while he unbuttons my jeans and pushes them off, taking my panties with them. He gets his pants down far enough to release his hard length and pushes into me slowly, unable to wait any longer to be together. Leaning into my ear, "Did I tell you how much I missed you when you were gone? I was miserable without you. I couldn't sleep and I didn't want to get out of bed." He moves with need as he glides his hands over my body, appreciating my curves. "My house felt dark and empty, just like my heart. I needed you to burn through all the bullshit in my life and show me how my life could be." He kisses me tenderly and I feel his breath hitch. He leans his forehead to mine, "How our life together could be." He holds my face in his hands, gazing into my eyes like he can see our future together. "I love you, baby. There's nothing I want more than you here with me."

Tears roll down my cheeks while I absorb his tender words. Not a smart-ass thought in my head. "I love you. I'll always be here to keep your bed warm and your heart full." He smiles against my cheek and I'm consumed by his love for me "Kiss me and love me the way you do, show me you love me."

Our words cease and he pushes in deep at our connection while he kisses me. Moving slow with long strokes and sweet kisses, tugging at my lips. I'm still not used to this new, harder Mick. His body is rock solid and his abs are more defined. I'm exploring his new toned physique with my fingers. He deepens our kiss and moves faster, with a purpose and causing me to whimper on every pass. I hold onto him tight and begin to move with him, drawing a low groan from his lips. My arms wrap around his neck and our bodies move together, comfortable and familiar with each other and what we want. He drives into me harder and I scream out his name, pushing him for more when he wants a marathon. I dig my fingers into his hair and rub his head while I move my hips with his, pushed by his kiss and his need. I squeeze him and he's huge inside me.

"I have more for you, baby." He pushes in further, when I thought I had all of him.

"Oh, Mick!" I call out uncontrollably.

He bends me in half, bringing my knees to my chest, burying himself deeper and deeper. He's amazing, any deeper and his size will send me soaring. "I want you to have all of me. I need to be as close to you as I can get." He pushes further and harder, lifting my leg to his mouth and kissing me from my knee to my ankle. Hooking my knees with his elbows and bringing them to my ears while he kisses me. He slows his pace and builds back to his harder strokes as he finds his way deeper and deeper into my body and soul.

I cry out at our intense connection, "Don't stop, baby." Everything goes dark and I'm falling, completely focused on him as I tighten around him buried so far inside me.

His arms envelope me, holding me to him while he continues his actions. "I've got you. I'll always have you."

Mick

Robbi's moving in today. She's working and my crew is helping move her stuff. We went through her place together and marked things to go to our house, things to go to the thrift store and things that need to get stored. She already took over my closet when she moved in all of her clothes and shoes.

It's a step towards everything I want and what I think she wants, too. I don't want to push her too fast. I need to give her time before I ask her to marry me. One step at a time and let her adjust.

After everything is loaded. I do a quick run through for trash and checking for things we've missed. Her place is mostly empty, so what's left stands out. I grab a trash bag and pick up real quick, so it doesn't look like a sty when she comes back to do her last bit of moving and cleaning. Throwing out empty ice cream containers and soda cans that had managed to get hidden under furniture. Tossing out empty bags that were left places. Trash that blended into the walls when her apartment was full. I pick up a wrinkled brown paper bag off the counter to throw it out, but it isn't empty and the contents fall to the floor. I quickly pick it up to put it back where I found it and can't help but notice it's a pregnancy test. I check the bag for the receipt and she bought it this week. I put it back on the counter and leave it where I found it. We never talked about birth control. I assumed she had it handled, but I guess nothing is 100% effective. I'm not upset by it, actually the idea makes me smile. I can't tell her I found the test. She'll tell me when she's ready or if there's something I need to know.

Mick

Walking through our house with all of her stuff here. Thinking about what I discovered at her apartment. I want her to know we're permanent. I don't want her questioning us if she comes up pregnant. I want her to know I love her and want to be with her. I'll be ecstatic to be the father of her child, but I want her with or without it.

Mick - Do you have our Grandmother's wedding ring?

Dr PITA - REALLY?

Dr PITA - Are you going to ask her?

Dr PITA - That's so quick! I love it! So romantic! Why wait when it's what you want?

Dr PITA - I'm so happy for you!

Mick - I'm sorry I asked.

Dr PITA - Sorry :)

Dr PITA - I won't say anything.

Dr PITA - Yes, I have the ring.

Mick - When can I get it?

Dr PITA - Impatient? What's up?

Dr PITA - Shotgun wedding? Mom will be so happy!

Mick - No, not a shotgun wedding.

Mick - I want to be engaged in case something like that did happen.

Dr PITA - Oh, you are serious.

Mick - Yep.

Mick - I like the idea of a mini and if you tell mom, I'll kill you in your sleep.

Dr PITA - Yes, sir! I'll get the ring to you today.

Dr PITA - :) <3

My sister the PITA. Hhmph… I'm smiling like a fool at the thought of it all.

Robbi

I was worried that moving in with Mick would be a disaster, but I went for it. I want to be with him and I've never wanted a man this way. He's there for me and it's a new feeling in my life to have someone that I can trust and wants to do things for me.

He's been watching the games at the bar when he's off work

and I have to work. I enjoy knowing he's there, though I do get busy on game nights. Something about being able to walk by where he's sitting and high five him when our team scores—it's silly, but I like it. He's doing something at the station today, so I don't think I'll see him until I get home tonight. Home. It's the first time I've ever had a real one. I'm working the happy hour shift, so I won't be too late tonight.

The prissy brunette is in the bar today for happy hour and I've been considering what I could do to her drink. It's fun to think about even though I'd never do it.

I get distracted by sirens screeching and lights flashing everywhere outside the bar. I look out the window to see emergency vehicles blocking the street and I wonder what's going on. There's a line of fire vehicles leading up to the bar and nobody is getting out to do anything. The sirens keep blaring. It's dusk and the flashing lights shine with the darkness falling behind them. The ladder truck pulls into the parking lot and I wonder what's going on until a banner drops over the side of the truck that says "Will you marry me?" and Mick hops out of the truck with a bouquet of red roses. The emergency personnel stick their heads out to watch the event and see what happens. I scream and move towards the door, ready to run to him.

The brunette starts for the door, squealing and stepping in front of me. "OMG! He's here for me! I knew he would come back for me!"

I grab her by the collar. "You've got that wrong. He's mine and he only loves me." I shove her back into the bar and slam the door closed in her face as I run to Mick.

He kneels on the ground as I approach him and grasps my hand, "I love you. I always want to be with you. Please be my wife and let me spend my life making yours better. Robbi, will you marry me?" He holds out an antique diamond ring and I give my hand to him. He slides the ring on my left ring finger, it shines beautifully and the flashing lights gleam off it in reflection. It fits perfectly.

I look at him in awe, speechless and full of love for this man that has already made my life so much more than it was before him. He saved me and he's given me the best thing, him.

"Robbi, baby, are you going to answer me?"

Shit! "Yes. Yes. Yes! I want nothing more than to marry you. I love you."

He stands up and I reach around his neck. He picks me up and twirls me around. "Yes!" He yells out in victory.

The emergency personnel cheer and clap around us.

He kisses me and holds me to him while I wrap my legs around his waist.

I lean into his ear and whisper, "Are you okay with it being more than just us?"

He stops and pulls me back to look at me, "Always. Is there something I should know?"

"Not yet, but there have been a couple scares."

"You should share those things with me."

"What do you think happens when you don't use a condom?

"I figured you were on birth control. We've been playing roulette this whole time?"

"Yes."

"Fuck." He scrubs his hand over his face. "I didn't know."

"Now that you know, are you going to do anything different?"

"That depends. Are you ready for a mini us?"

"I knew I'd do anything for you from the moment I met you." I whisper in his ear, "I saw your dream with me in the pool with the mini us. It will always be us."

He responds without words. His hands and lips on me tell me everything, like they always have.

ALSO BY NAOMI SPRINGTHORP

An All About the Diamond Romance

The Sweet Spot

King of Diamonds

Diamonds in Paradise (a novella)

Star Crossed in the Outfield... coming in 2019!

Novellas and standalone novels

Muffin Man (a novella)

Betting on Love (Vegas Romance)

Just a California Girl... coming soon

Jacks!... coming soon

Other novellas and standalone novels

Confessions of an Online Junkie... coming soon

Finally in Focus (a novella)... coming soon

THE SWEET SPOT

AN ALL ABOUT THE DIAMOND ROMANCE

Can her baseball fantasy become reality, or will she strike out at love?

Rick Seno is a sexy warrior behind the plate in his catcher's gear. In control and calling the game for the San Diego Seals. He'd show me the same attention in my bed, if he was more than my imaginary baseball boyfriend.

I've worn a Seno jersey to every game since Rick became a big leaguer. It's silly. I'm almost a decade older than him. I don't compare to the flawless baseball skanks who wait for him at the player's garage.

But, what am I supposed to do when the All-Star of my dreams invites me out after a game?

I can't believe he wants me. Until tonight, I was completely content with my life. Now, I'm caught off base and I'm not sure I can make it home safe.

ACKNOWLEDGMENTS

Without my sister and crazy 2am phone calls, the world just wouldn't be the same.

Thank you Tonya for taking such great photos and letting me take part in the adventure with you!

To the romance author community, thank you for being supportive. I appreciate everything, including the comic relief and phone calls.

Thank you to my cheerleaders! Naughties, you make each day better.

ABOUT THE AUTHOR

Naomi Springthorp is an emerging author. Muffin Man is her fourth release. She's also writing other contemporary romance novels and novellas featuring baseball, Las Vegas, and more.

Naomi is a born and raised Southern California girl. She lives with her husband and her feline fur babies. She believes that life has a soundtrack and half of the year should be spent cheering for her favorite baseball team.

Join her newsletter at
www.naomispringthorp.com/sign-up

Made in the USA
Middletown, DE
30 June 2019